THE CASTLE MURDERS

Gary O'Callaghan

The

Castle

Murders

St. Finbarr Press

FIRST ST. FINBARR PRESS EDITION MARCH 1998

 Published in the United States by St. Finbarr Press.

Library of Congress Cataloging-in-Publication Data

Library of Congress Catalog Card Number:
98-96054

ISBN 0-9662344-0-5

St Finbarr Press
P.O. Box 13072
Mill Creek, WA 98082-1072

Cover Design: Chris Sharp
Manufactured in the United States of America

To Susan and all the people who supported this effort. Special thanks to Longueville House and to the Mukilteo Coffe Company for providing inspiring locations in which to write.

Other Works by Gary O'Callaghan

Caithrem Ceallachain Caisel

(A Play adapted from a translation of an Eoghanacht Poem in the Annals of the Four Masters)

CHAPTER ONE

The rain was relentless. It cascaded down the window turning the view of the street into a kaleidoscope drawing muted shadows down the wall. The room was as depressed as I was, a female reporter alone in a strange country. Dad was so excited when he moved to Cork. "My own people Punkin," he'd called me Punkin as long as I could remember. "Ever since your mother died I've wanted to come over, god I'm glad I did. You won't believe how great the people are, they have time for you." Well one of those people had enough time for Dad to bury him in the mud of the Backwater.

I still couldn't believe it. Dad had been after me to visit ever since he'd moved here. I was always too busy, starting a job, starting a new relationship, starting something. Now I had to finish something. "Death by person or persons unknown" was what the cops said. The locals had said he was killed by "The Ghost of Dromineen." I didn't give much credit to that, whatever it was they meant. Still more than one person had come to me at the funeral with that opinion.

Tomorrow I'd drive up to Mallow. They'd found him buried in the mud on the bank of the river alongside

Dromineen Castle. I couldn't imagine what he'd been doing there. That was an O'Callaghan castle. It had nothing to do with us O'Donovans. Maybe it did, I was so tired I couldn't think straight. The rain was getting to me. The dingy room was getting to me. God how I wished I'd come over, at least for a couple of weeks in the summer.

I needed to get some sleep. I'd left Portland early yesterday, my mind in turmoil ever since the phone call from Dad's neighbor, Mrs. Murphy. I'd caught the first plane out of Portland for New York and switched to Aer Lingus last night. Dead on my feet, I'd arrived early this morning and driven to Cork just in time for the funeral. I didn't even think about driving on the left until I left the funeral. All at once I'd become very nervous, and had barely made it to the hotel.

Hunger was replacing sleep as my first priority. I didn't touch the slop they served on the plane, and hadn't eaten since dinner, day before yesterday. I wandered out onto the street, no idea of where to go. The rain had turned to a purple, black mist, slanting down the buildings, playing hide and seek with the shops on the other side of the street. I turned right looking for somewhere to eat. I walked to the end of the street where it turned left at the river, with nothing in sight but buildings in the mist. There were no people on the street. Everything must close early, I thought to myself. Looking back up the way I came, I thought I saw lights where the street turned at the other end. I started back, my feet squishing in their shoes. This mist was penetrating. I should have brought an umbrella, but didn't even think of it in my hurry to leave.

On the corner of the building where I stood was a

street sign, "Grand Parade" it read. Some parade, just me and the rain. As I walked back, I thought of Portland for some reason. Cork wasn't much like Portland, but this rain sure was. I could have been walking up Pine Street towards Broadway for all I could see. Except, there would have been people on the street. As I reached the upper end of the Grand Parade, I thought I could see people on the corner. When I got closer, I saw a bunch of kids - punkers. They were standing outside a brightly-lit hamburger place. One of the kids in the back of the group was talking to a man who looked familiar, sort of. I couldn't place him. He couldn't be from Portland, not here, and I didn't know a soul in Ireland. Well, it would come to me but most likely he just resembled someone I knew.

Inside, I ordered two burgers and a coke. I took the food to a window seat and inhaled it. I looked out the window, up Patrick Street. A few cars drove by, their headlights dancing off the wet pavement. An occasional pedestrian walked by, hunched against the wet. I couldn't see the kids on the corner, but felt them, just the same. My eyes felt like they were full of sand, and as I watched the street through the window, I began to be drawn into the scene. My mind saw me walking in that thick drizzle. I could feel the wet on my cheek. My head snapped up, awake, back in here. I'd been dozing. I looked around to get my bearings, and noticed that the kid who had been talking to the man outside was ordering something at the counter.

Struggling to my feet, I turned to leave and saw the kid gulp down his drink. As I left, he slowly wandered out behind me. I don't know if it was because I was tired, or if my ingrained warning system was trying to tell me something. But, I could feel the alarm at the back of my neck. As I turned the corner onto the Grand Parade, the kid kept following. He didn't stop to talk with his pals. He seemed intent, not even acknowledging their comments. I quickened my pace, though I couldn't hope to lose him. I only had a couple of blocks to go. His stride reached out to match my pace. As I crossed Washington Street, I glanced behind. My alarms were going full tilt. He was right behind me. My head turned back. I was ready to run, and suddenly I was sprawled out, face down on the sidewalk. I had tripped over the curb.

"Lady, will I give you a hand?" my teenage shadow asked. "'Tis a fierce night altogether. You should mind where you're goin, so."

I gaped as he sweetly offered a hand to help me up.

"Mr. Cogan, the night manager, asked me see you back to the hotel, this being a foul night and all. But, I could barely catch up to ask."

Some alarm system I thought, and I did recognize the man who'd been talking to this kid, back on the corner. He'd been at the desk when I checked into the hotel. I thanked him, feeling more than a little foolish, and wandered back to the hotel.

Once in my room, I stripped and collapsed into bed. The thoughts of the last couple of days quickly faded into sleep.

CHAPTER TWO

A glorious morning. The sun bloomed in the room chasing out the gloom of last night. Looking around the room, I was surprised that what had seemed dingy last night, was, in reality, Victorian. The furniture was old, probably antique. But, everything was in good shape, highly polished, and ornate. The windows were tall, set deep in the thick wall, with finely carved casements. The heavy velvet drapes flowed out from under the valences, down the twelve-foot wall. They were tied back with elegant twisted rope, and mounted to the wall by brass medallions. I had been so tired when I got in last night, I'd forgotten to pull the drapes. I was glad I'd forgotten. Waking to this sun filled room was a great start for the day.

Time to get moving. I rolled out of bed, and walked across an old carpet to the bathroom. "Incredible," the bathroom was a marvel. The floor and half way up the walls were tiled in small, white octagonal tiles. The tiles were arranged in a larger octagon with a black tile marking each intersection. The fixtures were from last century. A giant, claw-footed bathtub stood at the end of the room, next to a separate shower stall, which was next to a maze of pipes that seemed to form another shower stall. Looking closer at this contraption, I guessed it must be some kind of full body bidet. All of the fixtures seemed to be carved out of brass. I took off my pajamas and turned on the shower. The shower- head was like the nozzle of a watering can. Hot, hot water streamed out of it. Oh! it felt so good to wash off the dirt of the last two days. I wasn't sure if I ever wanted to come out of the shower.

Standing under this waterfall of deliciously hot water relaxed me to the point of dreaming. My mind wandered over the last couple of days, the horrible news, the rush to get ready. Oh Dad, I'll miss you so much. You had such hope for Ireland, and now ... I was bawling. My tears running down my face, mixing with the water, down my legs, between my toes. Why! why to such a wonderful man. Well, I thought to myself. I'd better stop this now, or I'd spend the rest of my life bawling in this shower, half way round the world.

I stepped out of the shower, and pulled a towel off the rack. As I dried myself, I found that the towel was warm. The towel rack was some kind of a radiator to heat the towels, marvelous! As I dried off, my thoughts wandered back to Dad's murder. Why had someone killed Dad? He barely knew anybody here. He had what little cash he carried still on him. The killing didn't make any sense. The story about the ghost of Dromineen was obvious hogwash. But why, why? If I could find out what Dad was doing in Mallow, maybe I could make some sense of all this. I put on jeans and a blouse, and remembered to grab a sweater as I left the room. I had been warned that the weather could change in a minute.

The dining room was very dark and empty. There wasn't a soul in sight. I waited for a minute, and then just sat at the closest table. The table was set formally, with linen, many knives, forks and spoons. It all looked very elegant, and very deserted. After a few minutes a waitress appeared at the back of the dining room. She hurried over. "Am I too early for breakfast?" I asked. "Breakfast, love? No, but you're too early for supper, it being half eleven in the morning."

"What time did you say?"

"Half eleven, It's almost noon."

I must have slept most of the morning away. I hadn't looked at a clock. I always get up at six back home. "Well, can I get some lunch then, since I missed breakfast," I asked the waitress.

"Oh, I'm sorry miss, we don't serve dinner at all. The cooks have all gone until supper this evening. Do you fancy a fry? I could do that meself."

"That's very kind of you," I said, "But, what's a fry?"

"You know, rashers, and eggs and a tomato. Sure, and I could find some juice in the fridge I'd say."

"That sounds marvelous, if it's not too much bother."

"Bother? It's no bother at all. Can't send a guest out into this fine day with naught in 'em, so."

A fry was just what I needed. As I was wolfing down the meal, the waitress brought a cup of coffee and a pitcher of cream, real cream. I was pleasantly surprised at the coffee. It was very dark, and very good. While I was drinking the coffee, I thought about the day. I didn't have much of a plan. If I drove up to Mallow and looked at where they'd found Dad, maybe something would come to mind. Oh my god! I'd left the car in the street when I arrived last night. From the noise entering the hotel, it was obvious that the empty street of last night was in full use today. I jumped up and ran out of the hotel. The street was jammed with cars and people. My car was nowhere in sight. Towed away? To where?

I went back into the hotel to ask the lady in reception how I could find out where they had taken my car. She looked at me, surprised, and said, "Why wasn't Mr. Cogan after putting it in the garage for you last night?"

I looked at her puzzled and said, "I don't understand. Did you say that Mr. Cogan parked it in the garage for me last night?"

"Yes ma'am. He said you looked so knackered when you first came in, that he asked you for the key and had one of the lads take your car to the garage. Do you want your keys?"

When she said this, I remembered he had asked for the key. Boy, was I ever losing it. "Yes, I would like the keys," I responded. "And where is the garage?"

"Well now, If you would take this hall past the dining room and turn right after the toilets you'd be on Washington Street. Just next to us is the car park. If you'd ask the lad there he'd have your car brought out to you."

I thanked her and turned down the hall. I passed the bathrooms, and saw the back entrance to the hotel. Walking into the garage, I saw a young man stuck halfway under a car. As I walked up to the car, he slid out from underneath and stood, a pleasant grin on his face.

"You'd be wantin' your car, would ye," he asked.

"Yes please, It's the blue..." I started to say. But, he cut me off.

"Wasn't I after fetching it off the street for you. I know very well indeed which car is yours. Wait a tick while I wipe me hands, and I'll bring it to ye."

I handed him the keys, and he sauntered off.

"Where are ye off to?" he asked as he stepped out of the car and handed me the keys.

"I'm not sure," I said. "I think I'll drive to Mallow first and then decide where I'm going. Could you tell me how I get to Mallow?"

"I could, of course," he responded. "As you leave the car park you go out of town. As you pass Jury's Hotel you'll come to the University. Turn to the right as you come to the University and head back into the city. After a bit you'd turn towards the river and go to the new bridge. Take the bridge across the river, going up Shandon Hill. The way will be signposted."

I thanked him. Got in the car, and started to leave.

"Mind your driving," he shouted after me. "The traffic is desperate."

As I pulled out into traffic, I thought, "This driving on the left really isn't very hard. You're sitting on the right next to the centerline, and just need to keep that perspective." I passed Jury's Hotel on the left and had to stop at the next light. Across the street in front of me was a large Iron Gate. Shit, it was the entrance to the University, and I had to turn right across a lane of traffic. When the light changed, I gunned the car and whipped to the right. I could just imagine the words being used by the man in the car next to me.

Perhaps I was a little cocky? I slowed down and tried to figure out where to go next. Before I could decide the road ended in a "T." I decided to go left, and soon was at the river. I followed the river to the new bridge and crossed. As I got to the other side, there was a sign, a very small sign pointing to the left. This sign said "LIMERICK N7," and pointed to what looked like an alley. Into the alley and up the hill until I came to a "Y." I chose the right and started winding down the hill. This section of Cork looked very poor. The street I was on was lined with row houses and occasional shops. Most of them were not well kept, and looked very small. The streets were crowded with busy people, though. A lot of kids running everywhere, moms with their babies, men going about the day's business. The houses and shops looked poor, but the women all wore high heels, everyone looked well fed, and they all seemed very animated. They bustled from here to there, talking to everyone they passed. Maybe the area was just old. It seemed too active to be poor.

I finally came out on the road that I had driven on entering Cork. Turning left, I was soon winding my way into the country. Although this was the main road North from Cork, it was little more than a country lane. I didn't remember much of my drive yesterday, but I did remember these 90-degree switchbacks as the road crossed, and recrossed the rail lines.

Yesterday's rain had disappeared, being replaced with a Van Huygen's sky. I don't think I've ever seen anything quite like it. Large, brilliantly white clouds were racing across the deepest blue sky. The clouds' shadows were spotlighting the fields in dark sweeps. I was driving along the side of a valley, most of the way up the right side. Off to the left were many farms. Each farm's fields were colored with activity great squares of green, ochre, sienna, and yellow. The colors were made more vibrant as the clouds' shadows swept over them. It could have been the Willamette Valley back home, except, every few miles I could see the remains of another old castle at the top of a hill. Somehow the colors seemed more intense than at home. Maybe it was just last night's rain that made everything so clear.

As I drove out of a copse of trees the road widened into real highway. It was still only two lanes, but they were very wide with large red shoulders. The shoulders reminded me of Eastern Oregon with the red lava roads. There was very little traffic, an occasional truck or passenger car. There seemed to be more foot traffic along the highway. A man walking his greyhounds, even a horse drawn cart with milk cans.

Soon, I was driving down a gentle slope entering the Backwater Valley and Mallow. As I entered town, I came upon a traffic circle or roundabout as they are called here. I knew that I had to keep left and take the first exit. The hotel had drawn me a map. So far it was working well. The driving wasn't hard at all wasn't hard at all here in the country, but could be a bit dicey if there was any traffic. I crossed under the railroad-bridge as soon as I had exited the roundabout, and soon was out in the country again.

I was driving along the bottom of the Backwater Valley, on the right hand side, with the Boggeragh Mountains forming a backdrop to the valley on my left. The hills on the right side were headed with the mansions of the old Protestant landlords. Most were now the farmhouses of the Irish who had taken back the land after independence. I was looking for a castle along the river to my left. As the road passed the Mallow racecourse, it narrowed to pass through a wood. Coming out of the wood the road widened again, and the whole valley opened up before me. "Dromineen" one of the O'Callaghan castles stood in ruin along the far bank of the Backwater. Moody it was. Nested in a small wood at the bottom of the hill, at the top of the limestone cliffs of the river.

CHAPTER THREE

"Now another one," he thought to himself. "A papist, rapacious and nosy. Probably shrill voiced and big. A troublemaker, no doubt. Well now, we'll see who gets the most trouble." He adjusted his collar, once again. The Bishop should arrive at any moment. Once more he would have to explain why the books didn't balance. Soon, very soon, he would have to take more of the treasure. He couldn't keep cadging the funds at the church. The Bishop was already suspicious, and with so few people there wasn't much money anyway.

The Reverend Samuels paced about the room, nervous about the meeting with the Bishop. His study was the old library. It was at the front of the house with delicate hand carved walnut bookcases lining two of the walls. The ceiling was a masterpiece of cast plaster with a Waterford Chandelier hanging from the center of a cluster of grapes. The artisan that had created the ceiling had a keen feel for the plants that he had worked into the forms of the ceiling. The Vicar paused at his desk for a moment, glancing at the ledger. He then began his harried route about the room again, glancing up the drive each time he approached the windows. Disgusted with himself and his worry, he flopped onto his reading chair. As he looked around the room he could see the stains in the wallpaper from the leaks in the roof. He simply had to fix the roof if there was to be any chance of maintaining the house, so hardly won and now so close to ruin.

The Vicar swept the remains of his hair out of his eyes as he ruminated. It was very important that he maintain what was left of the original estate. Most of the property had been sold off. Originally they had to sell most of the estate to the locals. Then as the years went on, and the traitors became prosperous they wouldn't work the land on the Estate, even though they had been offered far more than they were worth to do so. His father had been unable to keep up with the work and had no choice, no choice, at all, but to sell off more and more of the land. They had to have enough to keep up appearances. The Vicar remembered his Father's humiliation as he was forced to sell their land to the gillies that had once been only good enough to work it. Well, they'd see, they'd see - the scurrilous traitors, he'd show them in the end.

His fury raised him to his feet, and he began his route once again. The beauty of the day outside did nothing to temper his mood. At least he no longer feared the Bishop's visit. His anger at the injustices suffered at the hands of the papists had cleared any fear from his mind. In fact he began to look forward to the visit. The man, after all, was no match for him

As he paced he became more certain that he could easily avoid the Bishop's suspicion. In fact, he wondered whether he had perhaps built in his mind a suspicion that did not exist. What had he said at his last visit? Something to the effect that they would have to review the figures more closely next month, that he was disappointed in what he had seen. Now, hadn't the Bishop only meant that he was disappointed that the amount coming in was dwindling, not that there was something wrong. Surely, that is what he meant. It was only his own fear of being caught that had made him think the Bishop suspected him of anything. Though, God knows he deserved the little bit he had taken what with all the work he did for the people. And hadn't his family supported the Church for many centuries, even if they had stolen from it? In fact they were the major donors when the Church itself was built, or at least they had taken great pains to leave the impression that they were making large donations. So, to take a little of that back, and not for anything personal, for the estate, for the family. It was only his due.

Resolved in his mind of the justice of his action, the Vicar eagerly waited for the Bishop. Relaxed, he tumbled into his chair and rang for the housekeeper. "Mrs. Ryan, please clear off the desk and bring my tea. Mind, the Bishop should arrive at any moment and I want everything perfect for his visit."

"Aye sor, and haven't I everything ready this past half hour."

As he waited for Mrs. Ryan to bring the tea, he recalled the Bishop's recent visit. The Bishop had been reviewing the books for the last few months. He had said he wanted to just quickly look at them because so little money was forthcoming from the Parish. He hadn't really looked at the details, or mentioned anything about entries being wrong. At least the Vicar couldn't remember him saying anything like that. If only he could remember exactly what had been said. And that damned American, O'Donovan, nosing around Dromineen. What had he been looking for? O'Donovan had been a policeman in America. Surely the Bishop wouldn't use an American. It was too senseless, there was no connection between Dromineen and this Parish, at least none known to anyone outside of the Vicar's family, and the Vicar being the only person left in the family. Nevertheless O'Donovan's snooping had worried him. When he'd asked O'Donovan what his interest was the man had been very vague. No, the Vicar had not liked having O'Donovan around at all. And now his daughter was here. He wondered how much the daughter knew. He'd have to arrange to meet her and see if he could discover what she knew about Dromineen. This could be a much greater problem than the Bishop and the books, if indeed that was a problem at all.

CHAPTER FOUR

I drove along the highway until I was almost opposite Dromineen. I pulled the car off into an area that was used to drive tractors onto the fields along the river. The gates weren't locked, so I opened the one on the right, went through, and closed it. As I walked closer to the old castle, I could see the Backwater River that ran in front of the castle. The morning sun reflected off the water lighting the limestone cliffs that held the castle. Dromineen was clutched in the dark shadows of the trees that engulfed both ends, with the light off the water flitting over the walls. After I reached the river, I could see the whole of the castle on the riverside. It really wasn't a castle at all. It looked much more like a very large stone house. The walls appeared to be in fairly good shape. The roof had gone, as had anything that was not made of stone. I couldn't see any way to get to the castle, short of swimming across the river. There was a stone bridge across the river about a half-mile to the East that I could see. I'll try that, I thought to myself.

Walking back across the field to the car, I noticed a herd of cattle off to the west. They seemed to be getting closer. As I watched them, they began to move faster. I started moving faster, and so did they. A few broke away from the herd and started running for me. I broke into a run, not at all sure of their intentions. I reached the gate just as the quickest of the cattle reached me. Through the gate we contemplated each other. Within minutes the whole herd had reached the gate. I reached through the fence and was thoroughly licked for my trouble. I felt a little silly. This obviously was not Pamplona.

I got back in the car and headed back towards the road with the bridge. The main highway was very wide with no traffic. The road with the bridge led off to the right. As I turned onto it, I realized I was back driving on the righı. I jerked the car back onto the left side of the road, and quietly thanked St. Christopher for keeping the traffic down. The corner that I had turned was hidden behind trees. If anyone had been coming down the road towards me I wouldn't have seen them. I pulled the car over, shaking. I'd have to be more careful. I was so intense on finding something here that I wasn't paying attention to what I was doing. I calmed down in a few minutes and took off again, On the correct side of the road this time.

Just after I crossed the bridge, a gravel lane led off to the right, back towards the castle. I turned down the lane, thinking to myself that driving on the left will be no problem now! I was not only driving on the left, I was driving on the right as well. I couldn't see to either side. The lane was lined with trees and shrubs. Soon, the shrubbery on the right gave way to open fields. Suddenly, turning a corner, the road stopped. Between the road and the river there were large reservoirs of water. I opened the car door and stepped out. Immediately I was hit with a sickly sweet smell. It came from everywhere, hanging in the air like a spider web waiting to tangle the next victim. I couldn't see the castle from here, and couldn't get any further in the car. I got back in the car, turned it around, and headed back out. The odor was quickly gone, but a mystery with a bad feeling. Somehow this was connected to Dad. I couldn't see how, but I knew it was.

I turned right, onto the road when I left the lane. I went for some time without seeing any way to go right to reach the castle. Maybe I should have gone up river and tried to get to Dromineen from there. Just as I had decided to turn back, I came to another road leading off to the right. There was a signpost marked "Glantane," pointing to the right. I couldn't believe it. We were from Glantane. Dad had bought his dream cottage there. Maybe the castle was just a coincidence. Whoever had killed Dad had done it there because it was so remote. Most likely they had met there by chance and the murderer had taken advantage. And surely, the murder had nothing to do with ghosts. I drove on towards Glantane. I would try and see Mrs. Murphy, Dad's neighbor. She said that she could let me into Dad's cottage. She also probably knew the way into the castle.

The road was not much different than the lane I'd just driven down. It was a little wider and paved, but still lined with shrubs and trees. The road quickly turned left. Straight ahead was another lane on the edge of an estate. Just after turning the corner, I passed the gates. They were very imposing, massive granite towers capped with 3 foot high carved acorns. The road was very level, but twisted back and forth. It was as if a line on a topographical map that connected the start of the road with Glantane had been chosen by whoever had designed the road. As I twisted back and forth, following the road, I would come on small stone buildings. Most were whitewashed with corrugated iron roofs, running with rust. They appeared to be farm buildings of some sort. Each stood by a metal gate that led to fields behind the hedges. It was a beautiful drive. The sun was peeking in through the leaves of the Oaks, Elms, and Beeches that line the road, casting the Hawthorns, and other shrubs with spots of bright light that flitted from leaf to leaf as the wind blew across the trees. I passed a small thatched cottage where the owner was working on the roof. He waved as I passed, craning my neck to take it all in. The stone cottage was on the road. It was whitewashed with red trim on the windows. His wife was leaning out of the half door, saying something to her daughter who was feeding the geese in front of the stone barn. I was driving too fast to get a better look, but promised myself that I would go back. I didn't think I would ever forget that peaceful scene.

As I drove, the road became straighter. The houses were closer together, and most of them were quite modern. A small sign on the right of the road announced that I was in Glantane. I didn't look all that different from a small farm town in Oregon. The road forked ahead. I was to turn to the left up the hill, if I remembered Dad's instructions. The house would be just up the hill on the left. A small fairly new cottage set right next to Mrs. Murphy's cottage, which would be to the left of Dad's place. I would stop at Mrs. Murphy's to get the keys. I had met her at the funeral yesterday. She was very kind and very good looking. Dad's letters had said that she was in her sixties, and looked like me. Her looks had shocked me. I didn't think she was a day over forty. In fact, when she had introduced herself at the funeral, I couldn't make the connection, except she had long hair like mine, was as tall as I, and looked very much like I remembered my mother looking. I had expected Dad's neighbor to be a wrinkled old person, sort of short, maybe with a cane and a shawl. She was, in fact, tall, with a great figure, long auburn hair, and brilliant blue eyes.

I turned into Mrs. Murphy's drive, and stopped the car. As I started towards the house, Mrs. Murphy came out the front door to greet me. "Colleen, I'm so glad you accepted my invitation. Do come in, and we'll have tea. You look very tired from the drive, come along now."

"Thanks, Mrs. Murphy. I am very tired, and tea would be nice."

I was struck by her resemblance to mother, and me, again. I could have been looking at myself in a mirror thirty years from now. We entered a hall and turned left into the living room. The furniture was fairly modern, most of it, and looked slightly Scandinavian. It was mixed with a few old comfortable pieces. . There were books everywhere. The room had a real lived in look about it. "Sit here Colleen, I'll only be a minute in the kitchen." I sat where she had pointed, an old wing-backed club chair. "Had you a good drive up from Cork dear," she asked from the kitchen.

"It was a very nice drive, Mrs. Murphy, but I wanted to look around Dromineen Castle, and couldn't find a way in. I tried to get to it through the field in front, but couldn't get across the river, and then I tried a side road, but it led nowhere."

"Well Colleen, Patrick, my son, or I can take you

over later, if your feeling up to it. He should be here any time now. And Colleen, will you call me Cliona not Mrs. Murphy. I keep looking about for someone else in the room when you address me as Mrs. Murphy."

"OK!" I said back to the kitchen. While I was waiting for her to return, I looked around the room some more. Most of the wall space was covered with paintings. They were all sizes, all with brilliant light and colors. The subjects of the paintings seemed to be of the same room, kind of a sunroom filled with plants. In each picture there were different plants, sometimes flowers, sometimes just the room with gardening tools, but always the brilliance of the light and its affect on the colors. They were very good.

Mrs. Murphy came back into the room carrying a tray. She sat the tray on an old, highly polished table that was just in front of me. "Now! will I pour for us Colleen?"

"Please do," I answered. It looked very good. There was a teapot, sugar, cream, two cups and saucers, as well as two tiny spoons. She poured us both tea, and passed me my cup.

"Now, Colleen. Do have your tea. It is a desperate drive from Cork with the condition of our roads. It must be doubly hard for you, having to drive on the other side of the road."

I laughed a bit. "I think I was just a bit cocky when I started up here. One man in Cork is probably still swearing at me. I do feel very tired. This is all so strange. Yesterday, no, it was the day before yesterday. Anyway, whenever it was, I was in Portland, wondering how Dad was getting on. Now I'm 7000 miles from home, driving in a strange country, and Dad is dead. I just can't understand it! Oh no, I'm sorry." I had started crying again. I buried my head in my hands and tried to get control of myself.

"Hello Mother. Whose auto is in the driveway? I almost hit it. I ...Oh, I s.s.see you're busy. I'll be in the library."

Cliona's son Patrick had come into the living room taken one look at my red eyes and tear streaked face, and beat a hasty retreat.

CHAPTER FIVE

The Bishop leaned forward, tapping his driver on the shoulder. "Now David, what do you think about the Reverend Samuels?"

"Well Bishop, he has his finer points, I'm sure."

The Bishop of Cork, a small rotund man, whose jolly demeanor belied a sharp intelligence and thorough understanding of mankind, chuckled and leaned back in his seat. "David, you are most diplomatic. However, at this moment anyway, I'm more concerned with those points of the Reverend's character, which one would not consider as finer. Have you any observations to offer?"

"On occasion, sir, he does seem to be above it all."

"Just so, David, just so. I am most concerned with that particular trait. His congregation is dwindling without apparent reason. I wonder if his superior attitude is felt by the congregation, and they simply leave? How close are we?"

"Another 15 minutes sir."

"Good, good. I am afraid that this tendency to be removed from us mortals has also lead the Vicar to consider me something of a fool. Which of course I am more often than I would wish, but, not in the way that the Vicar supposes. He has been hiding something from me, or rather in his arrogance, he thinks he is hiding something from me. I should like to give him the opportunity to come forward, and shall give him some time to do so. This visit should be interesting if not pleasant.

The car grew quiet as they dropped into the Blackwater Valley, entering Mallow. Quickly David navigated the car around the roundabout exiting west along the Backwater. As soon as they passed out of town they came to the gates of the Samuel's Estate. David turned across the highway and followed the gravel drive up the hill to the Manor House. As the car approached the front portico, the Bishop could see Reverend Samuels watching their arrival from behind the library curtains. David stopped at the portico letting the bishop out. He then drove the car around the end of the house to the stable yard in back.

The Bishop's knock on the front door was greeted by Mrs. Ryan. "Ah your worship you've come to see the master, no doubt."

"Mrs. Ryan it is a pleasure to see you again. But you needn't refer to me as your worship, I am but a Protestant Bishop tending to a very scattered flock."

"Bishop is it? You heathens use the same titles as the good Christians of this country?"

"Mrs. Ryan, we Protestants are Christians too."

"Are you now. Well I suppose you must be. If more of us were as good as yourself we'd be the better for it. You'd best come in. Himself is in a fair state waiting your arrival."

The Bishop followed Mrs. Ryan into the Library. The Vicar was posed casually against the window casement. The long drive up to the front of the house, and the valley beyond was framed behind him. "Your Eminence, how very glad I am to see you again, and so soon. Twice in a month is quite unusual. Everything is in order, I trust?"

"Quite in order I'm sure. I've only come for a brief visit, and to see if you have considered a course of action since my last visit. After all, it has been a fortnight."

"A fortnight, indeed! A fortnight, to change the habits of my recalcitrant parishioners. I still do not understand what it is you expect of me. Is it my fault if they decide to stop attending? Can I do anything to expand their little, ungrateful minds? I ask you?"

"Reverend Samuels, we went over all of this on my last visit. Of course there are actions you can take to bring back some of your flock. I certainly did not expect you accomplish their return in a fortnight. But, I do expect you to have some thoughts on how you might accomplish their return. And I expected you to have them within a fortnight. Now, let's see what ideas you've developed.

"Ideas, I have a great many ideas, But I am not at all sure that they would be of much use in dealing with these ingrates. They don't seem to realize how much they owe my family, the help that we have provided each of them in the past. I have tried, repeatedly, to illustrate to them just how beholding they should feel. And still fewer and fewer come to Church. Bishop, I most certainly would welcome suggestions as how to instill in these people a proper measure of loyalty."

The Bishop, listening to the Vicar's harangue thought to himself, "How did we ever ordain this man.

He has missed the point entirely. I'm not at all sure I can leave him in his position."

The Vicar, warming to his theme continued. "To illustrate my point, Bishop, I'll tell you what happened the other day. That fellow Jepson, the one with the fancy grounds in Castletowne Roche, stopped in only last week. Stopped in to complain about my sermons, I might add. No sooner had he entered my house than he became quite argumentative, accused me of trying to bully the whole congregation. Bully them indeed, I did no more than I should. I explained to him, that I was merely explaining to the congregation their duties to the Church, and to the Samuels, who for centuries had provided the Protestant community with leadership, and that each of them owed a great deal, indeed the very positions that they hold in the community, to us. Now I ask you, Bishop, faced with a congregation that can only complain when asked to do no more than their duty, what more can I possibly do."

"Vicar, I am quite taken aback at all that you have told me. I'm not in the least bit sure that I can offer any advice, in view of what you have just said."

"Quite so, Bishop, quite so."

"However, I think if we would take a walk together perhaps between the both of us we could sort things out a bit."

"I don't at all see how that could help, but if you are determined I suppose it couldn't harm. Will I show you the grounds?"

"That would be lovely Vicar. I'll follow as I have never had the pleasure of seeing your demesne."

The Vicar led the Bishop back into the hall where they both put on their coats. At the back of the hall there was a wide central staircase with a passageway on each side. The Vicar took the passage on the right, which led to a door. Through the door was a narrow hall filled with wellingtons, old coats, and plastic buckets of vegetables. They passed through gingerly and exited into the rear courtyard, which was squared in, by stables. They were in a horrible state, badly in need of repair. No longer did they house the animals of the great demesnes. "As you can see Bishop we are no more than a shadow of what this great house once was." This was said with some anger in his voice, which the Bishop did not miss, but he did not respond, thinking it better not to feed the Vicar's resentments further. They turned to the right as the passed beyond the stable buildings, and came to a fallow pasture. The field was lined with hedges and a bit of a rock wall. Trees grew along the wall forming small woods that was parted by a trail. The Vicar led them down this trail into the cool of the woods.

"Now," said the Bishop. "Perhaps we can discuss these parishioners of yours. Or perhaps I should more accurately say your reaction to these people. I think that you would do well to remember just how much these people need your guidance." The Bishop mentally blushed at his statement, but he could not think of another way to approach the Vicar. He certainly wouldn't respond to direct criticism.

"That certainly is true Bishop. My guidance is sorely required."

"There you have it Vicar. If you can provide this needed guidance using the examples in scripture, you might find that your congregation responds quite positively."

"I...think there might be a possibility, but, as I have said, I have told them, repeatedly of their duty."

"Ah, but you see Vicar, they want to be shown. They are so very dependent on you that they might well respond quite positively."

"Yes, yes, your point is well taken. Perhaps I could lead them a bit better if I incorporated some of your approach." The two men had stopped walking as soon as they had started talking. They had turned and began walking back to the house as they talked. As they reached the house they fell silent, and passed back in through the back door. "Reverend Samuels would you please be so kind as to notify David that I am leaving. I think, Reverend, that we shall have to spend a few days thinking about what we have said today. I do think we both have a clearer view of the problem, and the start of a solution." The Bishop turned to leave. As he approached the front door he turned to the Vicar. "Oh! by the way Vicar, the Archdiocese is auditing my Diocese. As soon as they have finished with my accounts I'll send them to you. We might as well start here." With that, the Bishop descended the steps, entered his car, and drove off.

The Vicar, visibly shaken with the Bishop's parting remarks, stumbled back to the Library. "Mrs. Ryan," he shouted, "bring me more tea. I must think this through, very carefully. It would be dangerous to retrieve more of the treasure, considering what happened to the American," he thought. "I don't know if I have any choice. The funds must be replaced now that I have so little time. Damn the Bishop, he must suspect something with this second visit, and announcing this audit just as he was leaving. If I'm careful I can visit Dromineen once more. If I'm very careful.

CHAPTER SIX

"I'm so sorry, Cliona. I don't seem to be able to stop crying. Was that Patrick I frighten out of the room?

"Yes, that was Patrick, my son. I am afraid that he is helpless faced with a crying woman. Will I bring you more tea?

"No, no, give me a second to collect myself. I feel so silly. I haven't stopped crying since I got to Ireland. I need to start dealing with the fact that Dad is dead. It still seems so unreal. It's not fair. He was so happy here, and really looking forward to his new life. Every letter he wrote went on at great length describing the country, how nice the people were, how wonderful you were.

"We were becoming very close, Colleen. I miss him very much."

"Close? You and Dad? I mean, well I don't mean to pry. But you mean you were more than neighbors? I know he wrote about you often, but..."

"We were becoming more than neighbors, I think. Your father was interested in art, in painting mostly. He had a good eye for quality. We spent a lot of time together. He was a quietly charming man, curious about everything. My interest in painting fascinated him. So often, men I've met were, at best, tolerant of my work.

"The lady's hobby you know." They would say. Not your father, he understood how important painting is to me."

This was just like Dad. He was always interested in what people felt was important. I took another look at the room. It was dominated by the paintings that were hung on the walls. I didn't know much about painting. Dad had taken me to the Portland Art Museum once a year, but I was more interested in boys and clothes. "Are all those paintings yours?"

"All but the one over the fireplace, Colleen. That painting is by Colleen Berwick, a marvelous painter whom I admire very much."

"They're very nice, Cliona. All bright, a rush of color, yet a sense of sadness." All at once I burst out laughing. "God, I sound like a wine snob - bright, but sad, with a blueberry nose. I can't believe I said that."

Cliona laughing in response said, "You did a bit, but I'm glad you like them. Are you feeling a little better?"

"I am. That helped."

"Now then, will you join Patrick and I for lunch. He's not at all as rude as he seemed, just very shy. We can talk a bit about your plans. Perhaps we can help, and we'll ask Patrick to drive you over to Dromineen after."

"I will, thanks. I think all this emotion has left me very hungry. But isn't it very late for lunch? Haven't you eaten already?"

"Not at all. We don't eat until mid-afternoon, and our dinners are quite late. I'll just put a few things together if you'll excuse me for a few moments."

While Cliona was busy in the kitchen, I got up and walked around the room. The mixture of modern and old furniture suited the image of her that I was beginning to form. I had hardly spent enough time with her, but she did seem practical and obviously was very talented. The far side of the room was lit with light from three tall windows that looked out into the yard. I walked up to the middle window to get a better look. The grass was neatly trimmed, bordered with well-tended flowerbeds. "Cliona, your yard is beautiful."

"My what, Colleen?"

"Your yard, the flowers are exquisite."

"Oh yes, the garden."

"You call your yard a garden? OOPS! sorry Cliona." I could hear her chuckle at that faux paux. "I mean we call a garden a yard." At that she burst out laughing.

"You are your father's daughter, Colleen. This conversation could almost be a tape. I think I was even in the kitchen at the time. We quickly declared a truce and spent quite a while explaining our differences in English. I am ready for you, so.

"I don't understand why we have different names for the same things," I replied. "It is the same language after all."

"The same in its origins, but quite different influences on it, I'd say. Our English, particularly in Cork, remained Elizabethan until quite recently. Irish, the Irish language I mean, is the strongest influence on our English. On the other hand, your English has been changed by many different cultures, the Germans, the Italians, the French, the Chinese, and us."

As she finished talking, Cliona came into the room carrying a large carved wood tray covered with food. She set the tray on a low table in front of the fireplace. "Now, I'll get Patrick and we can start on this." The tray held china and silver for three, a plate of small crustless sandwiches, a plate of sliced fruit, a pot of tea, a bowl of sugar, and a pitcher of cream. The china was hand made earthenware with an intricate border design.

Cliona returned with a tall, rumpled looking man in tow. He seemed to be holding back. Not at all pleased with the prospect of sharing his lunch. His expression puzzled me. I couldn't tell if he was annoyed at the prospect or frightened.

"Colleen, I'd like you to meet my son Patrick. Patrick this is Colleen O'Donovan."

"Hello Colleen, I'm pleased to meet you. Welcome to Ireland. I am most sorry about your father. He was a fine man." As he talked, Patrick came over offering both his hands. I gave him my hand and watched his face transformed with the warmest smile I'd ever seen. He was so sincere I felt that his expression, which had puzzled me, was actually compassion and sorrow. I couldn't help warming to him immediately.

We all sat around the table and Cliona began serving. "Patrick thought that if he took you to Dromineen right after we have finished eating, you would have a good chance to look around."

"I appreciate the offer, but couldn't you just give me directions?"

Patrick stopped eating and said, "I think it better if I take you, Colleen. The boreen leading to the property is hard to find and the man who controls access to the castle can be very hard to handle, a right bollux." With that Patrick turned to his mother and winked. A conspirital smile turned her mouth as she returned Patrick's wink.

"What's going on," I asked? "Am I missing something?" I wasn't sure they had understood me. I was talking with most of a bite of sandwich still in my mouth. "Excuse me," I said. A little embarrassed. "Did I miss something?"

"Patrick's my protector. Donal Kelly, the farmer who owns the land around Dromineen, has been courting me for I don't know how many years. He is, unfortunately, a very boorish man who equates acres of land with attractiveness. He was not at all fond of your father, thinking that your father was standing in his way. Never realizing, of course, that he had been standing in his own way these many years."

"Is he a violent man, Cliona? I mean could he have killed Dad out of jealousy?"

"He easily could have," chimed in Patrick. "He has a fierce temper and is a wild man when aroused. He is the only man that came to mind when I heard about your father."

I stood up, getting excited. " You really think he could have killed Dad? I still can't figure out what Dad was doing at Dromineen Castle. Could this Donal have lured him over and then killed him?"

"Colleen, Patrick, I don't think Donal could kill anyone. At least not plan to kill them. Patrick, you really shouldn't accuse him, you know."

"Now mother, I didn't accuse him. I simply said he was who I thought of when I heard about Colleen's father. I do agree with you mother. I don't think he is the sort of person who could have lured someone to a spot and then killed them. All the same, if he came upon someone who he hated and then got into a rage, he would be perfectly capable of killing them." Patrick finished his food, putting the remains of his sandwich on the plate with a professorial flourish. He looked a little pompous to me at that moment.

I was pacing around the room by now. "Have either of you gone to the police?" I asked. "Whether or not he lured him over it certainly seems that he might have killed Dad."

Patrick responded, "there is no need Colleen..."

"No need," I almost shouted. "What do you mean no need." I could feel my temper rising. "My fathers dead and!"

Before I could finish, Patrick got up, came over and gently put his hand on my shoulder. "Colleen, what we mean is that Jim Brosnan, the local Guard, will know all about Donal Kelly and your father. This is a small village and little escapes notice."

"Oh! I am sorry." I could feel my anger turn into a blush. He didn't seem at all pompous now. "I seem intent on embarrassing myself. You are both very kind. I have no business losing my temper with you. I think it might be better if we don't talk about Dad for a bit. I would be a better guest if I listened a bit more. Patrick, why don't you tell me about yourself, what you're working on. Dad did write to say you were a history professor."

Patrick smiled. "Why don't we both sit down while you finish your lunch. I'll be glad to talk about myself. I'm a lecturer at University College Cork. I'm working on a paper on the Battle of Knocknanuss. The battle took place in the Seventeenth Century just across the river. There is very little written concerning the battle, so I'm collecting the folk history of Knocknanuss from people in the area."

"Patrick spends a great deal of his time talking to people in pubs in the area."

"That I do, that I do. I am constantly amazed at the amount of information that has been handed down from generation to generation. Unfortunately younger people have no interest in learning all of this and it will soon be lost."

That reminds me, Patrick. Are you going to the Hooley in Cullen on Friday?

"Yes mother, I am. You might want to come along Colleen. It's great fun. Two bachelor brothers hold it in their small house. Neighbors from all over come to dance, or sing, or play music. Will you come?"

"I might, thanks, but Friday is too far ahead right now to know. I'd just like to find out more about Dad."

"Of course, of course. Just let me know if you want to come along."

"Colleen, when you're finished with lunch why don't you go with Patrick to Dromineen. He can drive you there and anywhere else you need to go."

"If Patrick doesn't mind, I'd like his help. I'm ready"

"Come along then, Colleen."

CHAPTER SEVEN

"Will I drive Colleen? I'm familiar with the way there."

Are you sure it's not too much trouble, Patrick? I hate to impose on you."

With that exchange of mutual pleasantries, we both wedged into Patrick's miniature Japanese car. Patrick looked like a contortionist as he carefully twisted his long legs into position and backed into the car. His knees seemed to come all the way up to his chin when he finally got in. He drove into the village and turned right, retracing my route. The car was very little with no back seat. It wasn't missing, it just didn't have one. It was sort of a mini-mini-van. The rear was filled with books and papers that slid from side to side as we sped around every curve in the road. Patrick apparently noticed my glances from one part of the car to another. "Don't I have a portable office, Colleen? What it lacks in organization is more than compensated for by the convenience of it."

"It must be very convenient, being always with you. But you seem to be refilling the papers on each curve."

"I am at that," said Patrick as he laughed. "But

sure its only reference material, the order of which I can never remember anyway. Now, I wouldn't be going to fast for you, am I? Will I slow down?"

"No, no, I'm OK. The way I'm jammed into this contraption the jolts make very little difference." I spoke with more assurance than I felt. Every bump in the road jammed the thin seat into my bottom, and the car tilted precariously around each curve. It seemed like we probably were going 50, on a road where I felt I was speeding at 30.

As the shrubbery whisked by, I took a good look at Patrick. He wasn't good looking. He was to weathered for that. I had noticed how tall he was when he came into the room at his mother's. He was lanky, probably skinny would be a better word, and rumpled. Boy, was he rumpled. His clothes hadn't been pressed for a very long time. They weren't dirty, but well worn. He was hard to read. I'd thought him to be fairly aloof at his mother's house. But, he seemed to have an aura of warmth and humor, here in his car. When he talked to me I felt I had his undivided attention. His eyes never left my face when he talked to me or listened to me, for that matter. Somewhat disconcerting considering he was driving down a narrow road.

I wasn't at all sure why I felt I had to see where Dad had been killed. What could I possibly find that the Police hadn't discovered? And, if I found something, what would I do? I didn't have an answer, but I knew I had to look.

We were just passing the estate with the giant acorns on the gatepost, when Patrick turned left up a gravel road, just beyond the estate. "Why do they have giant acorns on their gatepost?" I asked.

"Acorns? Where?"

"There, on top of the gateposts."

"Oh, those. They're pineapples, not acorns. When the Protestants built these giant estates it was common for them to follow English custom. The pineapple being a very exotic fruit in those days was a sign of hospitality. Hospitality amongst themselves, not us."

As Patrick continued up the road we passed between an old Church and a graveyard. Just as we passed the church Patrick jerked the car to the left into the bushes as a car that looked like a jeep sped past us on the one lane road. "Bejaysus, that eejit! Where's Donal off to with the divil himself chasin' him? Getting to Dromineen will be that much easier with him gone, anyway."

"Shit, who was that fool. He almost killed us." I was very pissed. My heart was in my throat. We had a very close call. If it hadn't of been for Patrick's quick reflexes this little car would have been a spot on the road. As Patrick pulled back onto the road I calmed down a bit, but my heart was still racing. "Do people around here normally drive like that?"

"They don't, really. Donal is like a mad bull when he's in a temper. He lashes out with little concern for anyone around him, or for himself, for that matter. I wonder what set him off. I pity the poor creature that caused the row. We'd best take advantage of his absence. He guards his property as if it were a gold mine." With that said, Patrick pulled back onto the lane and drove on, passing fields of stubble. I hadn't noticed, but the weather was changing. The sun was covered with gray clouds that were coming toward us. I could just see the top of Dromineen off to the right. Patrick pulled the car off the road into a field at a closed gate. "We'll have to walk from here," Patrick said. "It's not far, just up to the next gate and down the ditch to the ruins."

I unwound from the car and stretched. Ahead were stone farm buildings with corrugated metal roofs. Cows were milling about a feed trough. It had become colder, and the sky was now covered with dark clouds. I pulled my coat around me, and set off after Patrick, who was almost at the next gate. He waited for me at the gate and rather gallantly offered to help me over. "Thanks Patrick, I'm not used to such gentlemanly behavior."

"My pleasure, entirely, Colleen."

Are we in some Noel Coward play? I thought to myself as we began walking towards the ruins. True, I wasn't used too much gallantry. In fact, I wasn't used to any. I didn't think I invited it much. Growing up with just Dad, I was quite a tomboy. I couldn't be... no I'd just met him, and he wasn't my type anyway - all tweedy and intellectual. I put that thought quickly out of my mind.

We stepped through a small gap in the fence made of wood. It looked like a small stepladder that had been put there to keep cattle out and let people through. I looked up at what seemed to be a carved portal in the remains of a wall. Behind the portal were three buildings, mostly intact. The walls were complete, and had been patched. The window openings in what looked like the main building had carved lintels of the same material as the portal gate. The main building and the building just to the left were about three stories high. The building to the right had no windows, only a door facing the main building. None of them had roofs or floors. We walked between the main building and the one without windows, towards the river. As we came to the edge of the bank overlooking the river we could see the sight of crime tape along the top of the cliff. The tape went down the side of the cliff, about twenty feet, and formed a small circle around a muddy beach at the edge of the river.

A light rain started falling as I stared at the circle of tape below. I felt very strange. I shuddered and drew my coat around me tighter. My father had died there, in that circle of tape, in the wet, cold mud. What could he have possibly done to deserve that end? Patrick was standing a ways off to my right, politely watching, leaving me to my thoughts. He smiled slightly when I looked at him, nodding his head as if to say he understood my grief, and shared it. It helped. It helped a great deal. I had felt so alone.

I started climbing down the bank. I just had to see where they had found him. The rain picked up making the climb down slippery. I made it to the bottom without falling and carefully kept outside the tape. There was little to see an impression in the mud where Dad had probably lain. The rain was really coming down now, and the wind was blowing, getting stronger. I tried getting up the bank where I'd come down, but it was too slippery. I could hear Patrick shouting at me, but couldn't understand what he was saying. He was pointing to a wooded area at the end of the main building. I understood what he meant even though I couldn't really hear him. I worked my way over to where I could grab on to branches to help me up the bank. Patrick had moved over to the wooded area and was pointing to something and yelling. I could barely hear him over the wind. By now I was soaking wet, my feet covered in mud. I carefully picked my way up the bank using the trees for hand holds. When I was about halfway up I saw what looked like a trail. Patrick had started down with his hand stretched out towards me. It was a trail! As I stood up Patrick reached me, grabbed my hand and pulled me onto the trail. Just as he pulled me over to him my hands grabbed for some bushes and missed. I fell sideways into the bushes. If any part of me had been dry, it wasn't dry any more. I had landed on my side and couldn't get a foothold. It was too slippery. My hands groped for something to hold on to. Finally I grabbed at a strong looking bush pulling the top down towards me. As I stood I could see that it very cleverly concealed a metal grate covering a stone opening. "Patrick look here," I shouted.

"Colleen, come along you're thoroughly drenched. We have to get back to the car."

"Just a minute, Patrick. Come here and see this."

"See what?"

"Just come here." I tugged at his hand and he came down to me, and looked where I was pointing. The grate was completely hidden if the bushes weren't pulled aside. He went over to the grate and squatted in front. He reached out and grabbed the bars. The grate opened easily. Patrick closed the grate and stood with a puzzled expression on his face. "Let's hurry to the car, Colleen. We're drenched, the both of us. I think I know what that is. If I'm right, I owe you a great deal of thanks, indeed. Come along now and mind your step. I'll explain in the car."

We both stumbled up the trail, Patrick pulling me

along behind him. When we got to the top I pulled my coat up over my head and half ran after Patrick. We quickly cleared the first gate and were running towards the car when we saw Donal Kelly standing next to his car, which he had parked alongside Patrick's car. The storm was in full force now. Donal was yelling something at us that we couldn't hear. He looked very angry. Patrick steered me to the passenger side of the car and helped me in. "I'll talk to Donal Colleen. I'll only be a tic."

I settled into the car and started wiping the rain off my face. I wished I had a towel or something, but didn't. I could see Patrick calmly listening to whatever Donal was saying. He was gesturing wildly as he talked, and in a minute stormed off to his car. Patrick returned with a wry expression on his face. "That bowsie. It seems that he has just returned from mother's, pressing his suit, as it were. And has been rejected soundly for his efforts. I have been ordered off his land until time ends." Patrick started the car, turned it around and headed home. "Now, about that grate. Something puzzles me, but I think I know what it is. You remember me saying that I was doing research about the battle of Knocknanuss? Well the leader of the Irish was a giant of a man Alisder McDonnell. He was treacherously killed following his capture. Originally he was buried close to where he was killed, but about a year later the O'Callaghans exhumed him and brought his remains, with great pomp and honor to their ancestral tomb. There they buried him with the O'Callaghan Kings. No one knows where that tomb is. I think you have found the entrance. One thing that puzzles me though, the grate was oiled, and opened easily, as if it was used recently."

"Was the grate what you were pointing at and yelling about back at the castle?"

"No Colleen, no one could have possibly have seen that the way it was hidden unless they fell right on top of it, as you did. I was just trying to show you where the trail started."

CHAPTER EIGHT

Donal's car careened down the road towards Glantane. He hadn't even noticed Patrick and Colleen when he forced their car into the bushes. He was in a fierce rage. How could that woman refuse to see him! After these many years of attention, of gifts and flowers, only to be set aside like some rough culchie when that damnable Yank moved next door. Well, the Yank had been taken care of and wouldn't interfere with his plans for Cliona - couldn't interfere.

But why wouldn't she see him now? He'd called with an invitation to dinner. He didn't mind the cost, not really. She'd been very short with him, called him mean. A dinner in Mallow wasn't mean - a man did have to be careful with his money. He couldn't be driving off to some toff's place in Cork. Even when he said he'd take her to the Glenarbor Lodge, god what must a dinner cost there, she'd refused. She didn't want him calling on her. He couldn't let it go. He had to see her and sort it out.

As Donal's car sped along the road it started to rain, making the road slippery. His car started to weave from side to side forcing him to slow down. Still traveling fast he slid into Glantane cross, careening past his turn up the hill. Cursing mightily he skidded to a stop in front of Keogh's Pub. By now the rain was blowing sideways, the wind shaking the car. He dropped into 1st gear and wrenched his car back onto the road, heading up the hill to Mrs. Murphy's. He hadn't thought at all what he would say to her when he confronted her. In fact he was beginning to wonder whether this was such a good idea after all.

Approaching Cliona's driveway, Donal stopped the car, wondering what would he say. His anger was replaced with the fear of facing her. He felt more like a schoolboy trying to ask the school sweetheart to a dance. If only that bloody Yank hadn't interfered. Torn between leaving and confronting her, he switched the engine off and sat staring into space. What could he do? He had imagined Cliona as his wife for as long as he could remember. No other woman had caught his fancy as she had. And now, nothing? No chance whatsoever? It just couldn't be. Frustrated and confused, Donal sat, unaware that the Garda had pulled up behind him.

Garda Jim Brosnan got out of the squad car and walked over to Donal's window. He rapped on Donal's window, bringing him to with a start. As Donal rolled down his window, Brosnan asked, "Donal, why are ye parked here, across from Mr. O'Donovan's? You wouldn't be thinkin of goin in would ye?"

"O'Donovan's place?" Donal asked, perplexed by the question. "I'm going to see Mrs. Murphy, not O'Donovan. He's dead, altogether."

"Goin to Mrs. Murphy's is it? It would appear that you're not going anywhere at all. Mrs. Murphy's indeed Donal. What would a fine woman like her have to do with the likes of you?"

"Are ye not oversteppin yourself, Jim Brosnan." Donal felt the ire rise in himself again. That this young lad should question his word was intolerable. "Damn you Brosnan. I'll not have you question my word." As he was talking, Donal opened the car door and started to get out of the car. Brosnan placed a large strong hand on his shoulder and shoved Donal back into his seat.

"I'll have no trouble off ye, Donal. Be still, so! Now, what is this tale about Mrs. Murphy? As if a lady of that quality would have any time for ye."

"The divil take ye, Jim Brosnan." Donal, unsure of himself with the Garda, settled himself back into the car seat. "Aren't I after marrying her? In my own good time of course. And I'll thank you for removing your hand."

"Marrying Cliona Murphy, you're thinkin of marrying her? Still that would explain your dislike of the yank. Him being so close to her and all. If you're so close, why then are sitting out here and not in her Drawing Room? I'll tell you why, Donal. You're sittin here across from O'Donovan's, not Mrs. Murphy's. You're sittin here thinkin of goin inside O'Donovan's. You're sittin here afraid we'll find something incriminating. So here you sit - afraid, making up stories about marrying Mrs. Murphy, when a straight answer would have served you better."

Donal was afraid now, not of the Garda, not of being arrested. He was afraid of Brosnan repeating his claim to be marrying Mrs. Murphy. If she ever heard of it, he would be done for sure. He couldn't very well ask

Brosnan not to repeat it. That would ensure the telling. Maybe he should just leave, quietly. Brosnan wasn't a talker. If he left without a fuss Brosnan would only remember his tale of marrying Mrs. Murphy as an excuse for being there. Yes, that was it. He needed to leave now, before it got any worse. "If you're done vilifying me, Jim Brosnan, I'll be leaving."

"Aye, be off with ye, before I drown. And I wouldn't be repeating your tale of marrying Mrs. Murphy. You'll be taken for a fool."

Donal, greatly relieved, rolled up the car window, started the car, and sped off. He suddenly realized he was going in the wrong direction, be decided he'd go on through Glanmire and take the turning to Mallow.

His thoughts were very confused. Apparently the Garda suspected him of murdering O'Donovan. That was understandable. He certainly had not been quiet about his dislike of the man. And what was he to do about Mrs. Murphy? He'd thought it would be so easy, with the Yank out of the way. He couldn't just let it be, but had no idea how he could improve the situation.

As he passed through Glanmire he turned down the hill towards Mallow. The storm was in full force now, making it hard to see. He was driving much slower, picking his way carefully. The wind was lashing across the windshield, and he almost missed the turn to Glantane. He slowed to a stop after passing the turn, and quickly reversed the car and turned into the road to Glantane. He turned in again at Killshanig Church and started up the lane to his farm.

When he rounded the last corner he saw a car parked next to his gate. He could also see a man and a woman running across his field. "Damn trespasser," he muttered to himself. Donal parked his car next to theirs, recognizing the car as Patrick Murphy's. It was the last straw. He slammed open the door and charged Patrick. "What are the two of ye doing on my property? I'll not have it! Get off this very minute."

"Donal, I have always been welcome on your farm before. Why should I not be welcome now?"

"Wasn't I just after seeing your mother, and me with no more than a kind invitation. Only to be soundly rejected. Well, what's good for the goose is good for the gander." With that, Donal turned and stormed back to his car. Patrick, feeling a bit amused by the tirade, returned to his car and drove off.

CHAPTER NINE

As they retraced their route back home, Patrick was still chuckling from his encounter with Donal. "That's a fierce man altogether. Well then, will you be staying at your Dad's house tonight, Colleen?"

"I don't think I'm ready for that Patrick."

"You'll at least stay for supper then?"

"That's very kind of you Patrick, but I want to see the police in Mallow as soon as we get back. And then I'd better drive back to Cork so I can change out of these wet clothes. I'll probably be able to face going into Dad's after a good night's sleep."

Patrick had turned up the heat in the car, which was helping to dry us out, at least on the surface. We didn't seem to be going anywhere near as fast as we had been on the way out, but we were quickly approaching Patrick's house. I wasn't at all sure of what to ask the police in Mallow. In fact I didn't even know if they were the ones to ask. Probably the police in Cork would take over a murder investigation. I really hadn't accomplished anything at Dromineen, other than getting very wet. So, I had to try to get something done today.

"Colleen, that grate that you found - I think it

could be a missing puzzle piece. If you recall, I'm collecting the folk history of the battle of Knocknanuss. Allisder McDonnell, who was killed, led the Irish. Local legend has it that the O'Callaghans secretly buried him in their catacombs, where the O'Callaghan Kings are buried. Unfortunately, no one knows where that catacomb is, other than it is supposed to be under one of the O'Callaghan Castles. I am sure that you found the entrance. Although I'm puzzled that it opened with such ease. It is as if someone used it regularly which makes no sense whatsoever."

"You told me all of this, Patrick."

"I did?"

"Yes, when we first got in the car. Why is it so important?"

"By itself it may not be all that important. It may be no more that a very small piece of puzzle. On the other hand, the fact that the tomb is still used, if it is the tomb, and that no one seems to know about the tomb, indicates that it is a large piece of the puzzle. Just how, I can't imagine. Maybe I'll find out more on Friday night."

"What's happening Friday night?"

"The Hooley in Cullen. It's a grand party with dancing, storytelling, singing and stories. I'm hoping Molly Hickey will be there. She is a treasure house of local history. Her father, his father, and his father before him were the local Seanchi. You know, the storytellers that kept the local history alive. I'm very anxious to tell Molly about what you found."

"It seems a small thing to be so excited about, Patrick."

"A small thing? Well, I suppose it is in the end.

But, to an historian any discovery can be quite exciting. It is, after all, what draws many of us to the profession. You might recall, as well, that many important finds start with a small discovery."

As he finished, Patrick pulled his mother's car into his mother's drive and parked behind my car. He quickly got out and raced around the car to open my door. While the door opened, Patrick asked, "If you won't stay for supper will you at least come in and say good-bye to mother?"

"Sure I will, Patrick. I want to thank your mom for her hospitality, anyway." As we walked to the house, I glanced over at Dad's house and shivered. I'd have to go in sooner or later, but was strangely reluctant. I wasn't superstitious at all, but seemed - well I don't know what I seemed. I just didn't want to go in at all.

We walked into Cliona's entry hall to be greeted by her gasp. "My, my, but you two look as if you've been swimming, clothes and all. Come in now and dry out by the fire. I'll fetch a hot toddy for the both of ye. It'll warm your insides." With that, Cliona whirled off to the kitchen.

We went into the living room and both of us backed up to the fire. The warmth immediately relaxed me. I expected that big clouds of steam could be seen rising from both of us. Of course they weren't, but I wouldn't have been surprised if they had been. Cliona soon came in carrying three glasses on a tray. She sat the tray on a nearby table and brought two glasses to Patrick and me. "Now," said Cliona. "Drink these up the both of ye, before ye catch your death."

I gingerly sipped my toddy. I could feel its

warmth spreading inside. "This does hit the spot, Cliona. Thanks." I rotated myself in front of the fire while I drank my toddy. We all seemed to be in our own worlds. Patrick and I as we dried in front of the fire, and Cliona as she watched us, wondering what we had found. Eventually I snapped out of my reverie. "I must be off. I want to thank both of you for all your help."

"Colleen, won't you stay for tea with Patrick and I? You're not dry as yet. I must admit I am dying to know what you found at Dromineen"

"Thanks Cliona, but I can't. I still have to see the police in Mallow and then drive back to Cork. I really need to be going. We really didn't find much of anything at the castle. It was to wet to stay very long."

"You found that grate which may be important to me, although it has nothing to with your father. And mother, as we got back to the car, Donal met us. He was in a foul temper. Apparently you did not appropriately appreciate his invitation."

"That man is insufferable. I have never encouraged him."

"I still wonder if he isn't somehow wound up in all of this. Well thank you very much for your hospitality, Cliona. And Patrick, it was very nice of you to drive me around this afternoon."

"Not at all, Colleen," they said in unison. We all laughed. "If you'll bring me my coat I'll put it in the car, and thanks again for everything." We wandered out together. Cliona handed me my sodden coat, and I got into my car. I looked back as I drove off. Patrick had his arm around his mom and both were waving good-bye. I left with a very comfortable feeling - like I was a member of their family.

The road back was becoming very familiar by now, and in no time I was back on the Killarney road. I turned right and drove back into Mallow. At the roundabout I continued straight into the town. The road was very narrow and got even narrower as I approached the shops. Cars were parked on both sides, half on the sidewalk in some places. There was little room for traffic, but there was plenty of traffic. Cars wove in and out, passing each other with bare inches to spare. Undaunted, I pressed forward. After a few blocks there was a sign showing that the Garda station was up an alley to the left. I had to wait for some school kids coming down the alley before I could go up. After the kids passed I continued up the alleyway until I came to a large parking area behind the buildings. I could see the Garda station on the left at the back of the parking lot. I pulled my car into a parking spot just in front, turned off the engine and sat. Now that I was hcrc, I wasn't too surc why I had comc.

I got out of the car and walked across the lot to the Garda station. It was a modern building made out of sandy colored cement block and aluminum, with many large antennae mounted on the roof. Parked to the left of the front door were three small blue police cars. If they had been big Fords or Chevies this could have been the police station in Beaverton, Oregon. It could have been, that is, until I walked inside. No screams, no drunks, just quiet - it was more like a small business than a police station. There was a small foyer with benches along both walls. The room was divided into two parts, two thirds of the room was in front, separated by a low wall running from left to right. In the very middle of the wall was a tall desk with a large, very large, man in a blue uniform seated at the desk. His age was hard to determine, about middle aged I guessed. As I strolled up to the desk he looked up and smiled. No, looking at that smile he was not middle aged, not yet.

"And what could we be doin' for ye, miss?"

"I'm Colleen O'Donovan. My father was found below Dromineen Castle."

"Oh! That was a terrible thing altogether miss. Your father was a fine man. Many a pint we've shared. I live no more than a few houses further along your road, like. Your Da and I spent many hours discussin' the finer points of Irish politics. Now here I am blatherin' on. You have a seat over there and I'll bring you some tea." With this the fellow turned about and disappeared into the depths of the building.

I looked around the room. It was devoid of ornaments with the exception of a large portrait of DeValera on the wall behind the desk. His portrait was to be found everywhere. The Irish venerate him as the founder of the modern state of Ireland. This was a room for business, a no nonsense room. After sitting a few more minutes, the Garda returned with a tray, a tray - no less, with a cup, a teapot, a sugarpot, and a pitcher of cream. There was no table on which to put the tray so he set it on his own desk, and motioned me over. "The Superintendent will be with ye in a tic miss. Now, if ye'd help yourself here you can take the cup back to your seat and have a bit of a sip before he comes out." I did as he asked and returned to the bench. I perched quite daintily on the edge with the cup balanced precariously on my knee. After a few sips I found my head bobbing. It was like last night in the hamburger place. I really needed a good nights sleep. As soon as I talked to this fellow I'd head back to Cork, get dinner, and turn in.

"Miss O'Donovan?" A voice broke into my reverie. I looked up at the source. A very tall, well-built man stood over me. He was looking down with an official smile that managed to just be friendly. His uniform was immaculate. You could slice bread with the crease on his trousers. "I'm Superintendent Mundell, Miss O'Donovan. Can I help you?"

"Yes you can, Superintendent. I'm interested in finding out what progress you've made concerning my father's murder."

"Of course, of course. We have made good progress, considering the amount of time that has elapsed. There are a number of lines of inquiry that we are following."

"Could you be a little more specific Superintendent?"

"Not at this time miss. If I were to divulge information prematurely it well could alter the course of our investigation. Now if you would please leave a number where we can reach you, with the Sergeant, I think. We will keep you advised of our progress." With that his little smile vanished, he turned on his heel, and vanished into the back of the station.

"Pay him no mind, miss. He means well, but is very protective of our cases. What with Dublin Castle after the important ones, and all."

"What do you mean Sergeant? About Dublin Castle I mean. What does Dublin have to do with a murder in Cork?"

"Naught miss, we have the case well in hand. What with Detective Lenihan being dedicated to it, and the Superintendent himself involved, and all. It's no more that we're a wee bit sensitive. We like to keep the cases local since we are so much more familiar with the people in the area. But, every once in a while Dublin will send in their own people. Like your own FBI might do some of the time. Now, if you could leave me a number where we can reach you?"

"I'll have to call you Sergeant. I'm staying at a hotel in Cork tonight, and I am not sure of where I'll be after then. When I know I'll phone you and let you know where you can call."

I walked out the door and crossed the parking lot to my car. I drove out of the lot at the top of the Garda station. Quickly I was in a residential neighborhood with high stone walls on either side. I came to a T in the road and turned right towards Cork. Soon I came to another T as the road wound up a hill. I was unsure which way to go. There were two little girls playing by the side of the street. I rolled down my window and asked them the way to Cork. They looked at me and giggled, shyly turning back to the game they were playing. I asked again and they quickly gathered up their toys and rushed behind the safety of their gate, peeking back around the low wall to see if I was still there. Their mother, apparently amused by the incident, came out of the house and walked up to the car, a small grin on her face. "Now aren't those two enough to drive you to distraction?"

"I didn't mean to frighten them."

"Well of course you didn't. And they're not

frightened, just a wee bit bashful. Is it directions you're after?"

"Yes, thank you. I'm trying to get back to my hotel in Cork, and seem to have taken a wrong turn somewhere."

"No problem at all. Simply turn your car around and head back down the hill. When you come to a cross, turn to the left, and then turn to your right, and you'll be at the Limerick Road. Turn left there and that will take you to Cork City."

"Thank you very much, and say good-bye to the girls for me."

I turned the car around and headed back down the hill. Following her instructions, I was soon on my way back to Cork City. The drive back was quiet. I managed to stay awake as I drove, and thought about what had happened today. I really didn't know much more about what had happened to Dad, but I suppose I shouldn't have expected to find out much. Both Mrs. Murphy and her son were very nice. I looked forward to seeing them both. The police weren't going to be much help until they had the case solved, which is no different than back home. The Superintendent did seem a bit of a pill, though.

As I came to the hotel, I remembered to park in the garage. I left the car and stumbled on my way to the dining room. I knew I was hungry. I mean I didn't feel hungry. I was too tired. But, I knew I was hungry. So I would eat. I was surprised to see the same woman waiting tables that had helped me this morning. Or more accurately this mid-day. She was helping another couple, so I sat down and waited for her to finish. When she was done helping the other people she turned and saw me.

She flashed me an apologetic smile and disappeared into the kitchen. During the wait, I realized that I would be better off going to bed. The events of the day and the jet lag caught up with me. I got up and waived to the waitress as she came out of the kitchen, and hurried off to my room.

I turned down the hall and walked into the lobby, and punched the button for the elevator. I waited, and waited, finally it came. The ride to my floor seemed like a slow motion movie. When I could almost stand it no longer, the elevator stopped and the door opened. Entering my room, I could barely take the time to remove my clothes before I crashed.

CHAPTER TEN

The two men sat quietly absorbed in their own worlds. At another time one or the other might have been appreciating the magnificent view out of the library window.

The house, high on Montenotte, looked down on Cork Harbor. A riot of colors, from the gardens between the top of the hill and the river below, led the eye to the many ships at the ways in the river. But, David was busy handicapping the dogs for the race tonight, and the Bishop was, once again, going over his last meeting with Reverend Samuels.

The man was turning a marginal parish into an empty one. The Samuels had held the position of Vicar since the seventeenth century when they did some favor for Lord Inchquin. On the whole they were typical of their class, not given to modesty or compassion, but strong on duty. The current Vicar was arrogant and buried in the past. His attitude towards his parishioners did not encourage them to attend. It only put them off. And who wouldn't be put off by a Vicar, who felt that they all owed him homage. "David, how am I to convince Vicar Samuels that he needs to try to attract his parishioners to Church, not order them."

"What Bishop? I was busy deciding on how to make my fortune, and didn't hear you at all."

"How am I to convince Vicar Samuels to change his ways? I need to convince him to try to attract his people to Church, that ordering them to attend will not work."

"I haven't a clue, I'm sure. The man fancies himself a grand lord. He doesn't even consider himself Irish. You'd best remove him if you've any hope of maintaining Mallow Parish."

"I'm hesitant to take such drastic measures, David, at least not yet. He does have good qualities too."

"Such as?

"Well now, let me gather my thoughts. Vicar Samuels is a very good organizer. He has never refused any task at which I have set him. And he has done each very well, indeed."

"Yes Bishop he is tireless in his pursuit of duty, but his efforts lack the human element, you know?

"Often they do, David. But consider what he did for Mrs. Westropp when her husband ran off with his secretary and left her destitute. He paid all her bills, he found her a reasonable place to live, and work. And he paid out of his own pocket without blinking an eyelid. Remember what he did for the Burns children too. So he has done a number of fine things, in spite of his lack of charm. Perhaps he does do these deeds from a sense of duty, but he is not without his good qualities."

"Yes I suppose that he does. Still that doesn't solve the problem of attendance in his parish." I wonder, could you simply go to him and tell him what needs to be done? Explain it to him in some detail, like."

I suppose I must if anything is to change. I would certainly have preferred him to have developed his own ideas though. He can be very stubborn, and will most likely resist ideas from anyone other than himself. The problem is himself, I'm afraid, more than anything else. I am not sure that my suggestions, regardless of how well I put them, can do any good."

"There you are then. As I said you will have to replace him, so."

"Not yet at any rate. The Parish will stand him a while longer, I trust. As soon as the audit is done, I will visit and put my ideas, well, some of my ideas anyway, to him; and we'll see what happens.

CHAPTER ELEVEN

I slowly opened my eyes, and looked around the room. There was no sun streaming in the widows like yesterday. It was gray or raining outside. I stretched and slowly rolled to a sitting position, quickly gathering the covers around me. It was cold in the room. I glanced at the clock on the bedside table. It was just 9:00 AM. "Good," I thought, "I'll be able to get breakfast if I hurry." I peeled off my pajamas and hurried to the bathroom. When the shower was adjusted to the perfect temperature I stepped under the water. The warmth felt very good, though it still felt like I had stepped into an old car wash. Whoever had dreamed up this shower was a marvel. "I'd better hurry," I thought, "if I'm going to move to Dad's today." I washed, dried, and completed my ablutions, dressed and went downstairs. As I passed the desk I saw Mr. Cogan, the night manager. "Mr. Cogan, I'll be checking out after breakfast. I'm moving into my Dad's house in Glantane. I want to thank you for all your help the other night."

"Not at all, at all, Miss O'Donovan. It was the least I could do. Now can we help you at all today? Will I have your bags packed while your having your breakfast."

Oh no, Mr. Cogan, I couldn't bother you with that. I can pack them myself."

"Now, it's no bother at all, Miss O'Donovan. I'll have them at the front desk with your bill when you're ready."

"If you insist, and thanks."

"You're very welcome indeed."

Once again I had slipped into laying on the pleasantries. No harm, but I had a good night's sleep, so there was no excuse today. Maybe the graciousness that everyone was showing me had taken a few rough edges off. I walked into the dining room and sat where I had yesterday, hoping that the same waitress would be working today. I had been there only a few minutes when I saw her coming out of the kitchen. She had a gigantic tray on her shoulder. I couldn't see what kind of food was on the tray, but it had many meals on it. She flashed me a brief smile and hurried off to deliver the goodies to a family seated in the back.

While I was waiting for her to come over and take my order, I looked around the dining room. It was dark and elegant, in a very old fashioned way, probably Victorian, just like my room. As opposed to yesterday there were quite a few people eating. There was only one other waitress, so they both were very busy. Most of the customers appeared to be business people, with the exception of a couple of families. The people looked different, not in any specific way, just different. I probably stood out like a sore thumb. The women were all better dressed than I. They all had dresses on, and high heeled shoes.

I thought that I would take my time driving to Glantane. I really had little to do. I wasn't looking forward to moving into Dad's. Going through his things was going to be very painful, but it had to be done. Maybe I'd drive into Mallow when it got to me and give the phone number to the Garda, and find somewhere to have lunch. Maybe Patrick would be around and we could go together. He was very nice.

"Miss O'Donovan?"

"Oh, yes. Nice to see you again." My waitress from yesterday stood at my side with menu offered, and a very welcoming smile on her face. "I don't think I need a menu. A fry will do nicely. By the way, what's your name?"

"Brid, miss. It's an old Irish name."

"It's lovely Brid. If I can call you that."

"Oh you can indeed. We're not formal at all."

"No you don't seem to be. In fact you seem friendlier than us Americans."

"Not at all, miss. You Americans are the friendliest people I've ever met. I always look forward to meeting Americans. Those German businessmen over there? They're so stiff, and they're mean."

"How Brid? Do they talk abusively or what?"

"No, no miss. By mean, I mean cheap. They watch their money very closely. And the French, they always complain about the food, so. Not you Yanks, you're always smiling, and so appreciative of anything I do. Well, listen to me blatherin on, and you sittin there with naught to eat."

With that, Brid turned, and hurried off to the kitchen. I'd always heard about how much Americans are disliked oversees. Certainly I had seen none of it in Ireland. Just the opposite, I had been welcomed very warmly, with the exception of the Superintendent in Mallow, and that had nothing to do with my being American.

Brid delivered my breakfast with a smile, and I dug in. I hadn't realized how hungry I was. It seemed like I couldn't get it in fast enough. Whilst shoveling I wondered how long I should stay in Ireland. I would like to stay until the police had resolved Dad's murder, but I knew from my experience as a reporter in Portland that it could take months, if the murder could be resolved. There didn't seem to be much for the police to go on, or at least I didn't see much. The police hadn't really told me anything. They could have a suspect right now for all I knew. With the exception of my job there was little rush to get back, and I'm sure that work didn't expect me for a couple of weeks. So I would stay for a couple of weeks or until the police had something definite.

That decision made, I felt better. I didn't do well when loose ends were flying about. I finished my breakfast, retrieved the car and repeated the route I took yesterday. Except I didn't turn directly in front of other cars like I had yesterday. My driving had become quite good, if I say so myself. It wasn't really raining. It was an Oregon mist. Enough though, so that I had to turn the wipers on. The trip into Mallow went a lot faster than it had yesterday. What had been a rainbow of colors yesterday was now a gray inkwash. I negotiated the roundabout in Mallow with skill and headed West towards Glantane.

As I approached Dad's house I started feeling a

little reluctant to go in. For some reason it seemed that once I entered the house I was accepting Dad's death. I slowly pulled into the drive and parked in front of Dad's house. I noticed that Patrick's car was in front of his mom's house. This made me feel better. There would be someone understanding around if it got to be too much for me. I got out of the car and walked up to the front door. The door was unlocked so I went in. It was dark inside. I could barely see. All the curtains were drawn. I groped along the wall for a light switch. My hand finally felt a switch. I turned it on and was greeted with a mess. The living room was a shambles. The furniture was overturned, all of the books had been pulled off the bookshelves and dumped helter skelter on the floor.

I stood there, dumbstruck. Who could possibly have done this? Why? This was just too much! I was so pissed I was shaking. I turned on my heel and walked next door to Mrs. Murphy's. I began hammering on the door, which was quickly answered by Cliona. "Colleen, what ever is the matter that you're knocking in my door?"

"Oh Cliona, this is unbelievable. I just went into Dad's house. Someone has turned it upside down. It's a horrible mess."

"What do you mean, turned it upside down?"

"The furniture is torn apart, all of the books are pulled out of the shelves and strewn around the room. I didn't go any further into the house, but I imagine that the rest of it is a mess too."

"Did you notice what they took? No, no you wouldn't have if you didn't go through the house. We had best call the Garda right away. Now, come in and have a sit. I'll bring you a whiskey and then call."

"Yes, call them please. You know, I don't think I'll find anything missing. This has to be connected with Dad's murder." I followed Cliona into her Living Room and sat in the nearest chair. I really wasn't ready for more surprises. I had begun to cool off, sort of. I started having crazy ideas as I sat waiting for Cliona to bring me the drink. Could one of the crooks Dad had put away in Portland have followed him to Ireland? Or maybe have moved to Ireland when he got out, and then when he saw Dad in Ireland it became too much for him, and he did Dad in? No, that was crazy, more than a little far-fetched. But everything was so strange; Dad just wasn't the kind of person to get murdered. He was quiet and kept to himself.

"Colleen?"

I looked up. Patrick stood there, a concerned look on his face and a drink in his hand. "I'm so sorry. Is there anything I can do to help?"

"Hello Patrick. For a start you could hand me that drink."

He chuckled and handed me the drink. "Mother says the Gardai are on their way. They have asked that none of us go back into the house until they are finished. They are treating it as if it was connected with the death of your father."

"Are the Gardai any good Patrick? The Superintendent wouldn't give me the time of day yesterday. He seemed to really resent me stopping in to see how the case was going."

"On the whole they are quite good, I'd say. The Superintendent is another matter now. Not that he is'nt competent, mind. It's just that he's is a different sort. I don't think he was pleased to be transferred to Mallow. The talk is that he expected a promotion to Dublin, but some way or another ended up here. We don't really know much about him, even though he has been here for over a year. He is not married, apparently has no friends or interests outside of his work. I am not at all surprised that he paid you short shrift. Detective Lenihan, on the other hand, is a good friend, Colleen. I'll keep you abreast of things."

"Thanks Patrick, that will help a lot. None of this makes any sense to me. When I get this way, feeling useless I need to do something, anything, or I feel like I'll explode. I was going to start going through Dad's stuff to see if I could find anything that would give me some idea what he might have been doing. So I could somehow relate something to his murder. I think I'll have to wait a while now. How long do you think the Garda will be?"

"Oh, they should be here any minute now. It's not far to Mallow."

"No Patrick. I mean how long will they spend in Dad's house?"

"I don't know I'm sure. This is all a new experience to me. Will you sit? Mother is bringing in tea."

"Thank you. I might as well relax. I don't think I'm going to get into the house for quite a while. I do wish they would get here, and start. Did they actually say that they thought this has something to do with Dad's murder?"

"No they didn't say that. What they did say was that they were treating it as if it were connected to your father's murder. Quite a different thing altogether." Until they have the opportunity of investigating the house they can't really come to any conclusions, I wouldn't think."

While we were talking, Cliona had come into the room carrying a tray, once again, filled with goodies. She sat down across from us and passed out cups and saucers. Remaining on the tray was a bowl of fruit and plates of cookies. "Now, what will each of you have? Some biscuits Colleen? They are home made and quite good. They are Patrick's grandmother's famous recipe."

"Didn't she win a prize at one of the Cork Exhibitions for the recipe mother?"

"She did indeed Patrick."

"No, just tea for me, please. I had a big breakfast at the hotel. Well, maybe one, they do look very good."

"And you Patrick?"

"I'll have a biscuit with my tea, mother. Thank you."

I sipped my tea, quietly. What they call a biscuit, I call a cookie, and it was very good. I wondered if I would be allowed to move into Dad's house, or would the police tape it and seal me out. I don't know if I really cared. I wasn't all that excited about moving in, not after this latest bit. Actually, I thought I really did want to move in, to have something normal happen. Even if I had never been in the house, knowing that Dad had lived there, and seeing his things would make it the closest I could get to normal. Maybe what I really meant was familiar not normal. Patrick and Cliona seemed to also be lost in thought. A line from an old Platters song floated through my thoughts "Lost in my reverie."

I could hear cars coming up the drive, their wheels

crunching the gravel as they drove up. The sound of doors opening and slamming shut was followed by the sound of footsteps in the gravel, and then a knock on the door.

"I'll get it," said Patrick as he rose from his chair. He walked down the hall and opened the door. We could hear Patrick say, "Hello Liam. We were just talking about you, come in, and welcome." I heard a lovely light voice answer. "Thank you very much indeed Patrick. I will come in. Is the young lady who was in next door here at all?

She is Liam. Her name is Colleen O'Donovan. Her father is the man found at Clonmeen Castle.

Actually it was at Dromineen, Patrick, and I had deduced that she is the daughter of Mr. O'Donovan.

"Dromineen? Of course it was Dromineen. Did I say Clonmeen? In any case, she and mother are in the drawing room having tea. Would you care to join us?

"That is very kind of you, Patrick. But I must steal Miss O'Donovan from you and take her next door. Perhaps when we're finished."

They both walked into the Drawing Room. Liam was a small very dapper man in his mid forties. He was wearing a very conservative suit that looked like it was tailor made. His hair was dark and curly and slightly long. He didn't look at all like a cop, which was probably very handy for a detective. Patrick introduced us, "Liam this is Colleen O'Donovan. Colleen this is Liam Lenihan." Liam came over and shook my hand.

"Miss O'Donovan, I wonder if I might steal you away over? I'd like you to show us how you entered the house, and what you did when you got in. I'm sorry to bother you but it is important."

"It is no bother detective, officer? What should I call you?"

"Liam would do well indeed, ma'am."

"Good Liam. Then you can call me Colleen please." He turned and left the room. I followed. We walked across the drive to Dad's. Just as we were about to enter, Liam turned to me and asked, "Now. Colleen will you please go up to the door just as you did earlier, and go in the same way you did then." I walked up to the door, reached for the doorknob, turned the knob, and walked in. "The door was unlocked Colleen?"

"Yes it was Liam. I didn't think anything of it at the time. I don't know if Dad normally locked the door or not. Maybe Mrs. Murphy knows. Dad certainly never left the door unlocked at home, though." I walked through the entry into the living room and stopped. "I only came in this far, Liam. I looked around at the mess and then left. I was only here less than a minute."

"You didn't draw the drapes?"

"No, I touched nothing."

"So you have no idea if anything is missing or not?"

"No, sorry."

"Don't be sorry. We can take a look later, after the crime lab people are finished. That's all I want for now Colleen. Could I ask you to wait until were done here? It would help a great deal."

"I don't mind at all Liam. I'm not going anywhere. I came here to move in." I walked out and started back to Cliona's. Liam came out and motioned to a group of people with cameras and valises. They started towards Dad's as I walked back into Cliona's. Both Patrick and Cliona were at the door. I suppose I didn't hear them clucking as they marched me back to the living room. But, I did feel well cared for, between the two of them.

"Do you think they will be long mother," asked Patrick.

"I haven't a clue, I am sure Patrick. This is altogether a new experience for me. I can assure you."

"Yes. Well then, here we are, so. Colleen, will I top up your whiskey?

"What Patrick? Oh no, I think I'm fine. If you don't mind, I'll just sit here quietly until they are done next door." At that they both turned to each other and quietly carried on a conversation, the subject of which I remain unaware. It isn't that I didn't want to talk to them. It is just that I wanted to be alone with my thoughts, to get in touch with my feelings. Damn, what a load of bull. What I wanted to do was think about the break-in next door. See if I could make any sense out of it. So I didn't have much information. That hadn't always stopped me before.

All of a sudden I wanted to get in to see if anything was missing. Unfortunately I probably couldn't tell if anything was missing since I had never been in that house before this morning. Still, I wanted to get in there. I got up and excused myself. I walked next door. There was a cop standing at the front door with a foreboding look on his face. I flashed him my friendly but lost smile, which caused him to step in front of me as I started to go in. "Would you mind officer?

"Ah now, I'm not an officer at all miss, no more

than you. And what is it that I should mind?"

"I can't get in with you standing there - Uh, what do I call you? I'd call you officer. That's what we call cops in the US. But, you didn't like that. So what do I call you?"

"Gard, ma'am. Were referred to as Gards, in the odd few moments of politeness we occasionally experience." And I am well aware that you cannot get in, as you put it. Detective Lenihan's instructions ma'am. No one Dennis is to be comin in the house til I give instructions. He was after tellin me most emphatically. Now if you'd care to return to the Murphy's, I'll let you know when Detective Lenihan is ready for you to go in."

I was turning to go when I heard Liam calling me from the front door. "Colleen, could I ask you a few questions?"

"Sure, Liam. What can I help you with? Should I come in the house?"

"No, not yet Colleen. Were not finished photographing and taking fingerprints. Let me come out to you" He walked slowly over to me, a puzzled expression on his face. "Do you have any idea what your father might have been working on?"

"Working on? What do you mean? I don't think Dad was working on anything."

"I'm not at all sure what I mean, Colleen. The only two rooms that seem to have been disturbed are the drawing room and the library. The library is the worst of the two. There are papers strewn all over. They look like your Dad was taking notes for research."

"Oh that. Dad had written some time ago that he was going to write about the history of the bagpipe in

Ireland. They fascinated Dad. I never did hear whether he had actually done anything though. So I don't think I can be of much help. Which brings up another subject. I couldn't wait to get over here to help see if anything was missing. But I can't really help. Except for the minute I was in the house a little while ago, I have never been inside. I have no idea of what Dad kept here."

"You haven't visited your father before?"

"No. He's only been here a year."

"Sure and you'll be no help at all with this. Sorry, I mean you'll not be able to help us identify what's here and what isn't. Except there seem to be a few pages missing from your dad's notes." He appears to have numbered the pages"

"How very like Dad. He always said the only reason he was a good cop was the notes he took. If it will be of any help I'll look over Dad's notes."

"That might help, Colleen. I'll bring them over when were finished here." He then turned and walked back into the house.

CHAPTER TWELVE

I had been back in Cliona's house for over an hour before the Garda finished and Liam returned. Cliona, Patrick and I had done little more than engage in small talk. I was getting nervous about something, or maybe apprehensive. It didn't make much sense, but I was on edge. I wondered if I just wanted to have the cops leave, so I could move in. Probably.

Liam came in with papers in his hands. "Colleen, could you take a look at your father's papers, like? These are the ones with pages missing."

"Sure Liam, I'll look at them tonight after I've moved in. When will you be done?"

"We'll finish in no more than a few minutes. There was not much evidence unless we can identify strange fingerprints. Mind you, we do have another line of inquiry. Cliona, are you and Donal Kelly getting married anytime in the near future?" That got her attention.

"Marry Donal Kelly. "I'd sooner marry a snake than that oinseach. What ever put that idea into your head Liam?

"Garda Brosnan found him parked in his car

across from the house yesterday. As you might imagine we are keeping a close eye on Mr. O'Donovan's house. Jim was suspicious. So he went up to the car and questioned Donal. His story was that he and you were to be soon married and that he was here to see you."

"Well, as you might imagine, Mr. Kelly and I are not getting married. Good Lord the idea is preposterous. And he was never here yesterday, Liam. He did call however. And was very strange, I might add. I angered him I'm afraid."

"You did, mother. Colleen and I were almost killed by him driving out when we drove in to Dromineen. He was still angry when he came back as we were leaving."

"How did you know he was angry, asked Liam?"

"Colleen and I were walking back to my car having been at Dromineen, when Donal came driving back. He parked next to my car and had a few words for me as I walked up to the car. You know Liam, he was here quite a long time. Colleen and I were at Dromineen for over an hour. It takes no more than fifteen minutes to drive to Glantane. Another fifteen to drive back leaves at least a half an hour for Donal here. You didn't see him mother? Not even briefly?"

"I didn't Patrick. After he called inviting me to dinner I went into the back room to stretch a canvass. I got rather involved and didn't come out for a couple of hours. He could have done as he wished without me being any the wiser."

I remembered what Patrick had said yesterday about Donal's temper. "Isn't this important Liam?" I asked. "After what Cliona and Patrick said yesterday, you know, about Donal being jealous of my father; His being here yesterday must be important."

"Well it might Colleen. But you must remember that we checked the house as soon as we had identified your father. It was not like it is now at all. So there has been adequate time for any number of people to have entered and ransacked the house. Cliona, have you noticed any one at all in the house next door?"

"I'm very sorry Liam, but I haven't. I have been in and out every day so I most likely wouldn't have seen anyone. And even if I was here, there would have to be quite a racket to get my attention. Sorry"

"Not at all, Cliona. We don't expect every detail to neatly fall into place. Colleen, don't be discouraged. We do have some promising lines of inquiry. And though Donal's presence here yesterday certainly is not proof of his being in your house, it is an interesting coincidence that bears investigation. Now if you will all excuse me it is time to return to the office and continue that investigating. Colleen, I'm sure you can go in now."

Liam left. I waited a second or two and then excused myself and went next door. As I walked over the police cars were just leaving. They had left the front door ajar so I went in. The mess that had greeted me in the living room had been straightened. I wondered if that was common for the Garda. It certainly wasn't back home.

I walked through the house looking at each room in turn. It was a lovely cottage. Dad had furnished it quite attractively. Actually Cliona must have been responsible for the furnishings. Dad's taste was all in his mouth. No, that wasn't fair. He had very good taste. It's just that he never did much about it. The furniture looked old, but looking at it together it was quite nice. The second bedroom was bare with a few boxes of god knows what stored in it. I didn't bother to look to see if it was Dad's stuff or things left behind by previous owners of the cottage. Dad's room was typical of him; a big bed with what looked like a down comforter. Not a lot of decoration. One painting was on the wall by the door. It looked as if it might be by Cliona - a landscape full of color, post impressionist really. There was nothing else on the walls in the room. The starkness of the room highlighted the single painting.

I moved on to the kitchen. It was a good size room with an old table in the center. The table was well worn with many years of use. In fact I wouldn't be surprised if the top hadn't been worn enough from meal preparation that it was no longer level. On the back wall facing the house was a very large metal contraption that looked like it might be a stove. There were two large Chrome lids with wound wire handles that looked like giant waffle irons on top. There also were three doors in front that looked like ovens. The whole device gave off a gentle comforting heat. I liked this room. I really liked this room. I could feel that Dad had spent a great deal of time in here.

At last I went into the library. Liam, or another of the Gardai, had straightened most of the room. Or at least I thought they must have, since there was little mess any longer. I sat at Dad's desk and took a look at Dad's papers that Liam had given to me. They seemed to be in chronological order. The last page before the missing pages was about a composer "Turloch O'Carolan" dated in the early 16th Century. Then came the missing pages, four in all. The notes then took up again in the late 17th Century. Whatever was missing must have taken place in the middle of the 17th Century. "Brilliant Watson," my Dad would have said. Liam surely would have figured this much out. I decided to return to the living room and straighten up the remains of the mess there, since my brilliant bit of deduction had not solved the case.

Instead of cleaning I sat in the living room unwilling to get my things out of the car. That would mean making room for them, which meant cleaning out at least some of Dad's things. This was going to be very hard. I sat there, immobile until I heard a soft hello from the front door. I turned my head and saw Cliona with a handful of boxes standing half in half out of the door.

"I don't at all want to interfere, Colleen, but I wondered if I could take a few of your father's things out in these boxes. No more than enough to make room for you, mind. You could always go through them later."

"Cliona that is the kindest thing anyone has ever done. How did you know how much that would bother me? Please come in. I'll just wait in here if you don't mind." It was no more than ten minutes when Cliona came back into the living room. "I've packed up two drawers of the bureau and half the amoire, Colleen. It will have to do for now. I'll send Patrick over to fetch everything." With that she left rather hurriedly. Oh my god I thought to myself. I wasn't very sensitive. Cleaning out Dad's things was hard on Cliona too. I should have realized. I felt like a shnook. I barely noticed Patrick coming in, and then leaving with many boxes. He smiled wanly as he trudged by with his load of grief.

After a while I settled down and went into the kitchen. If I was going to stay here I needed to check the food supply. There was a small fridge under the counter. It contained little other than one bottle, a glass bottle yet, of spoiled milk and some cheese covered in plastic wrap, one egg and a few rashers. I took the milk and looked for somewhere to dump it. Under the sink was the usual garbage pail, in it went. The cupboards had dishes and serving pieces and pots, but no food. There was a back door. Maybe there was a pantry on the way out. I opened the door, bingo. Well, sort of bingo. There was one box of cornflakes in the cupboard. I definitely needed to go to the store. I wasn't sure how long I would be here, but even if it was only for one night, I needed to go to the store.

I didn't know where a store was. I didn't know when the garbage would be picked up. I didn't know if the garbage would be picked up. What about the phone, the lights? I probably wouldn't be here long enough to worry about them. What about the house? It hit me again that I now had a house in Ireland. What on Earth was I going to do with it? I decided to solve that problem later. I got up, went to the car, and brought in my suitcase. Cliona had come back and was in the bedroom loading the last box from Dad's dresser.

"Here Colleen, give me your things. I'll put them away for you in your Da's bureau. You get yourself off to the drawing room. I'll join you shortly."

"Thanks Cliona," I said meekly. I went back into the living room and sat, waiting for Cliona to finish. I wondered how long I would stay in Ireland. I hadn't thought about it much. I knew I wanted to find out what had happened to Dad. That could take months. I didn't think I had the resources to stay that long. But, I couldn't see leaving without knowing what had happened. I had better be prepared to stay for as long as I could. For right now I needed to prepare to stay the night and get some food. "Cliona!" I shouted into the back of the house. She appeared at the door to the living room, carrying the last box of Dad's things.

"Will I put these down or can I take them over and come back, Colleen."

"Oh I'm sorry, Cliona. I didn't realize you had your hands full. I just need to do a little food shopping and wondered if you could tell me where to go."

"I can indeed. If you'll give me a minute, I'll take these over and then go with you."

"Cliona, you've been so much help I can't keep asking you to do things for me."

"Not to worry, Colleen. I plan on taking advantage. I am not fond of driving. If I can impose on you and have you drive, I'll take you to the best shops."

"Great! I'll be happy to drive, if you don't mind placing your life on the line."

"I'm sure your drivin is better than mine. I am not usually timid, but cars frighten me and I poke along aggravating everyone. Let me take these things over, and I'll join you in a few minutes."

Cliona finished packing the last box and left. I went into the bathroom to freshen up, and was surprised to find it very modern. Dad must have had it completely redone. The floor was tiled with a typical bathroom tile, as were the walls. There was a separate shower and a large tub. The sink was on a pedestal though. It would not be as convenient as one in a cabinet. I looked into the mirror over the sink and was surprised to see that I looked quite normal. I didn't feel the least bit normal. I fussed with my hair a little, but on the whole I was ready to go.

I walked out to the car to wait for Cliona. She was not long. She quietly got into the car, and we took off. As I approached the "Y" at the bottom of the hill I slowed not knowing which way to go. "Cliona, where are we going?"

"I'm sorry. Turn to the right. We'll drive into Mallow. There's a super market there that should have most of what you're looking for. "

"Cliona? I'm sorry I wasn't more sensitive back at the Dad's house. I think I was so wrapped up in my own loss I didn't think that it was painful for you too."

"That's kind of you to say, Colleen. Perhaps I should explain a bit."

"No, no, you needn't explain at all."

"I'd feel better if I did. You see Patrick is what we call a love child. His father and I were madly in love. We acted with great abandon our short time together. He was killed just after I became pregnant, and never knew of Patrick."

"Oh I'm so sorry, Cliona. I had no idea."

"Of course you didn't. We've only just met. Let me finish. I have had a marvelous life, and known many wonderful men. None of them could ever come close to Patrick's father though. That is until I met your father. He is the first man since Declan died that I started to feel at like I did those many years ago, and then he died. It has made me very sad."

"I don't know what to say. I am very sorry for both of us." Cliona didn't respond. She had a far away look on her face, and seemed to settle deeper into the car seat. After that our drive was uneventful. I was getting used to the driving, and the road was becoming familiar. As we reached Mallow Cliona directed me to the supermarket. At the roundabout we went around half way and exited into the town. We passed a large Dairy on the left, and then turned right onto a street that went below the town. No sooner had we turned a corner than we came to a large park on the right. The park was along the Blackwater River. It had playing fields, play equipment and a large grassed area. I was so busy looking at the park that I almost missed the supermarket, but I didn't.

I was surprised by the market. Except for the prices you could barely tell you weren't at home. The prices did seem higher and the checkers sat on stools. What a great idea. I had spent my days as a grocery checker standing all day, destroying my feet. I picked up some basics while Cliona shopped. We soon were back in the car and headed home.

"What are your plans now Colleen?" Cliona asked as we headed home. She seemed in a very good mood, in spite of her revelation.

"I don't know. I was thinking about it this morning, but I couldn't decide what to do. I know I would like to stay to see if the police catch Dad's killer. But I don't know what I'll do if that takes a long time. The murder doesn't seem to make much sense, and the police seem to be, well slow. No, that's not right. It's not the police. It's me. I want the case solved by tonight, and they obviously aren't going to do that. I guess, to answer your question, I'll stick around awhile. I have vacation coming at work, so that won't be a problem. At least not for a while."

"I think that the local Garda is very good, Colleen. Liam is very successful. If there is anything to be found out he will find it out, I am sure. Now, since you're staying for a while why don't you join Patrick and I in Dublin? We are taking the train up tomorrow and spending the night with my Aunt Maude, who is an amazing character altogether. Patrick has research to do at the National Library. You and I can take in the sights while he's working away."

"You are too much, taking me to the store, and now this. But, it does sound inviting. Thanks, I'd love to come along. What time do we leave?"

"I'm so pleased you'll join us. We'll leave the house at 10:00. Just bring casual clothes, and - No we'll do the town, bring one nice frock too."

CHAPTER THIRTEEN

I finished my dinner and quickly cleaned up. I had cooked a simple dinner of Quinsworth fish and sautéed vegetables. All things considered, it had been quite good. An idea had come to me while I had been eating. Since I had little or nothing to do for the evening, and since I had really made no progress discovering Dad's murderer, I could help Patrick. He had been quite excited about my discovery of the opening below the castle. We hadn't had enough time to explore it. I could easily go back tonight and poke around to see what I could find.

Of course I would have to be very careful. Donal Kelly wouldn't welcome me any more than he did Patrick. But, if I was very careful I am sure that I could get to the castle unnoticed. I'd have to park my car at the abandoned church at the start of Donal's property and walk in. If I kept to the fence and went along it to the river, I'd be next to the castle, and could easily climb the fence where it went into the trees. Donal couldn't possibly see me unless he was out walking around the castle. I'd have to leave the car behind the church, just in case he was driving in or out.

I looked around the kitchen for a flashlight. I

found a fairly new one in a cupboard in the pantry. I was starting to get excited now. This would be a lot of fun. I really needed something to take my mind off of Dad. I stuck a pen and a notepad into my purse. I could write down everything I saw in the cave. Patrick had said that the man from whatever battle he was studying was buried there along with the O'Callaghan Kings. I wondered if I would see a bunch of old bones or would they be in coffins. Well it didn't matter. It wouldn't bother me to see the bones. Maybe there would be armor and swords. I really didn't know how old kings were buried.

It was dusk by the time I got out of the house. I turned the car down what were becoming familiar roads. As soon as I got out of town it became quite a bit darker. The trees overhanging the road shut out what little remaining light there was. It was a night you could imagine that bats were flying around. They probably were out every night, here in the country. Its just that tonight, with the quiet dark, the headlights of the car reflecting back from the hedges alongside the road, seemed a little spooky - appropriate for bats.

I slowed down after a while. The road was not lit, and I was afraid of missing the turn. I wasn't sure that I could see the pineapple gate unless I was moving fairly slow. The road seemed strange at night. It had started to become familiar during the day, but at night it seemed like a new road. Turning a bend I was blinded by the lights of an oncoming car. It was past me in a flash. It must have been going over fifty. I had to stop the car for a moment while my eyes readjusted. I started out again, even slower. Driving was not turning out to be as easy as I had first imagined. I soon reached the gates with the pineapples. I turned up the lane just beyond them, and turned into the Church's drive. I parked the car out of sight of the road, and got out.

The lane up to the castle was hard going at first. It was in the trees around the Church and very dark. I didn't dare use the flashlight in case it could be seen from Kelly's house. I stubbed my toes a few times, but soon I came out of the woods to where the lane went through fields. I could easily see where I was going now. There seemed to be lights to the left at the top of the hill. They were flickering on and off irregularly. It confused me at first, until I figured out that it was from a house in the trees, and that the flickering was from branches blowing back and forth. I started up the hill and was soon past the house in the trees. I had been a little frightened of being seen when I walked directly in front of the house. I felt like the lights from the house had lit me up like a beacon, but no alarm had been raised. After passing the house I could see where the fence went down to the castle. I angled off through the field partly to shorten the distance, and partly to make sure I wouldn't be seen from the house. I did not want to meet Donal Kelly out here alone at night. He seemed to me the most likely suspect, and if so what might he do to me if he caught me snooping around the site of the murder.

I really hadn't thought about that possibility when I started this adventure. Now that it had occurred to me, I started feeling a little apprehensive. This probably wasn't the brightest thing I had ever done. However, it would be brighter if I hurried on to the castle where I couldn't be seen from the house. I could move quicker through the field, and did so. I came to the fence and followed it down to where it was next to the castle. There was a gate sort of a thing in the fence for people to cross, so I clambered over. I was back in the woods that were on both sides of the castle. It was dark, very dark.

I was feeling strange since I had thought about the possibility of Donal actually being the murderer. This dark wood wasn't helping one little bit. I came to a stone wall that must be part of the castle. I followed the wall towards the river. Thankfully I was going very carefully. The stone wall was part of a building that ended at the edge of the cliff above the river. I stopped and turned back the other way. I had to feel my way along the building. It had become very dark. Even though I was moving very slowly, I stumbled a lot.

As I turned the corner of the building I came to an open area, a courtyard really. Looking across into the woods on the far side of the castle, I thought I could see movement in the shadows. Boy I was letting myself really get spooked. I moved along the building that was also the East end of the castle. I was moving back towards the river. It was lighter here on the inside of the castle courtyard. I looked back over to the other side, looking for whatever it was that I had seen. The main part of the castle was in the way. I couldn't see the woods on that side. The main building of the castle was blocking what little light there was. I slowly worked my way to the end of the building and stopped when I reached a short wall that was on the top of the cliff over the river, and ran between the two buildings. I tried to get my bearings. I knew I was above the grate and to the East of it. I looked over the cliff to get a better view. I had to strain to see much of anything, but I thought I saw the trail that we had been on, and I also saw that movement again. I knew what it was, just the branches of the trees moving.

Relieved at that discovery, I decided that it would be safe to turn on the flashlight briefly. I didn't think there would be any chance of being seen from the house with both the woods and the castle in the way. I quickly found the trail. It was further off to the left than I remembered. In fact it was at the far side of the castle. I turned the flashlight off and started working my way back so that I could go around the end of the castle. To get around the castle I had to go out of the courtyard I had been in. There was a tall gate carved in stone set in the remains of a wall. I passed through and turned right towards the far woods. I was a little hesitant to enter the woods, in spite of my logical explanation of things. But I pressed on. The branches brushed against my face as I looked for the trail that we had come up earlier. I was starting to get a little wet. The leaves had a little of the rain that had fallen on them earlier. This adventure was losing its imagined attractiveness.

A few more steps into the woods, and I finally came to the trail. I wondered if I could turn the flashlight back on. Surely Donal couldn't see it way over here. I decided to leave it off. Why take a chance I could see better now that I was on the trail. While I was working my way down the trail I got the definite impression that someone was beside me in the woods. I even thought I could here someone moving. I knew better. It was just the setting and the dark night. Still, I was really getting the willies, and I kept looking over my shoulder.

The trail was getting steeper, and I must have looked back once too often. I found myself face down on the trail, slightly bruised, and my pride greatly wounded. What a dumb thing to do. If I had only kept my eyes on where I was going, I wouldn't be rolling about in the muck. I looked back at the rock I had tripped over, cursing it soundly. It didn't look quite right. Maybe it was a branch or something, Without thinking I turned the flashlight on and pointed it. Oh my God! It was Donal Kelley's head. He was lying just off the trail facing back towards his house. I scrambled to my feet and ran like the four horsemen were after me. I suppressed a scream, and thought, this isn't right, he could be alive and might need my help. I stopped and forced myself to go back. I went over to him, a sinking feeling in my stomach. His head had been bashed in just like Dad. I reached over to feel his neck to see if there was a pulse. There wasn't. His head and neck were covered in blood, which got all over my hand. It was very warm. He must have just been killed.

The noises, the movement in the trees, that must have been the killer. It was obvious that Donal had not been killed by a fall. The queasy feeling in my stomach got worse. I had to get out of here. The killer could be watching me right now. Well using the flashlight was no problem. I scrambled back up the trail as quick as I could. As soon as I cleared the woods I ran with abandon towards Donal's house. I expected the killer was running behind me, about to catch up. I stole a look back and didn't see anyone. I slowed a little, but kept on towards Donal's house. As I got closer to the house I could hear a dog barking, furiously. When I got there I could see a sheep dog tied to a tree. The dog was barking for all it was worth, and strained at the rope. He paid no attention whatsoever to me, so I went to the front door and knocked. I had no idea if anyone lived with Donal. I wanted to use the phone to call the police, but didn't want to barge in on someone.

After knocking several times without getting an answer I went in. No one in Ireland locked their doors it seemed. The phone was in the hall as I entered. I didn't see a phone book, nor could I remember the number for The Garda, so I dialed the operator and asked for the police. The man that answered didn't sound familiar. I asked for Liam, but was told that he had left, so I explained to the man what I had seen. He became very officious, in a kindly way. He said he would send people up right away, and that I was to remain where I was. I went into the living room and sat and waited.

CHAPTER FOURTEEN

In no time at all, I saw the lights of approaching cars bouncing off the walls. There were no sirens or flashing lights, but they were arriving quickly. I went to the door and saw two police cars pull up. As soon as the first car stopped the driver jumped out and ran around the car to open the door. No less than the Superintendent stepped out. I felt I was watching a movie of a Graham Greene novel, but quickly found out that I was in the movie, not watching it.

The Superintendent had a funny look on his face as he approached me. "Good evening Miss O'Donovan. Perhaps we could step inside for a moment, and you can tell me what this is all about." As he was talking, he firmly grabbed me by the elbow and tried to guide me inside. It is not in my nature to be manhandled, not by anyone. I wrenched my arm out of his grasp and said, "Superintendent, we can talk right here, and please do not ever grab me again." I could feel the red rising in my cheeks.

"I will grab whoever I need whenever I need when I am investigating a possible murder." The Superintendent's voice had risen considerably. "Might I remind you that you are at the scene of a crime, at night, with your hands covered with blood." "At night? What difference does it make that I'm here at night," I yelled at him. I couldn't think of anything else to say I was so pissed at him. He turned and asked the Sergeant to come over. When the Sergeant got there the Superintendent said, "If you'll deign to tell me where we might find the body I'll instruct my men. "He's lying in the trail on the West Side of the castle," I responded.

The Superintendent walked over to the second car and spoke to the men who were standing about it. One man came over to me while the others opened the trunk and took out cases. The man approached with an apologetic look on his face. "Miss, the Superintendent has asked me to take a sample of the blood from your hands." I started to explode, but didn't. It wasn't this fellow's fault that he worked for a jerk, and what difference would it make anyway. No one would seriously consider me a suspect. I held out my hands. As he daubed some of the blood off my hands I said, "By the way, I didn't have a chance to tell the Superintendent, but I thought I heard someone in the woods beside the trail. It most likely was the killer. I am sure he's far away by now, but you never know."

"Yes miss, in the woods you say?"

"Right next to the trail sergeant. He was in the woods next to the trail just before I discovered the body." Donal was now "The Body." Well he might as well be. He didn't seem to be a very pleasant person, and more likely than not he killed my Dad. Strangely, I didn't feel satisfied that he was dead, nor relieved that the killer had been brought to justice. I just felt numb, and a little confused at the Superintendent's attitude. While I was busy musing I noticed that the Sergeant had gone over to the Superintendent with the sample. The Superintendent glanced at it briefly then turned to another man and handed him the blood. All the while he was talking to the Sergeant and looking back and forth between the Sergeant and me. A moment later the Sergeant went off at a trot, apparently to the castle. The Superintendent started walking my way.

"So now we have a mysterious stranger lurking in the wood. Is that it Miss O'Donovan? And can you describe him?"

"You needn't be facetious Superintendent. No I can't describe him. I didn't see him at all."

"If you didn't see him how do you know it is a man. As far as that goes how do you know that anyone at all was there?"

"I, uhm, well I guess I don't know it was a man. I just assumed that it was. What I really saw was movement in the trees and I had the feeling of a presence. I suppose it could have been no more than my imagination."

"What I think, Miss O'Donovan is that it is your invention, thought up at the spur of the moment to throw suspicion away from yourself."

"What! Of all the idiotic ideas!"

"Let me finish, if you please. You obviously invented this story. You mentioned none of this when you called. It only came out when it became apparent that you were under suspicion."

"This is really absurd! What possible reason could I have for killing this man? I just arrived in this country two days ago. I never met the man, and have only seen him once at a distance. Well, twice if you count tonight." In any case I did not kill him, and you have no evidence that I did."

"We shall see miss. We shall see. I think that we had best continue this discussion at headquarters."

"Headquarters? Are you arresting me?"

"Not at this time, Miss O'Donovan. Now if you will wait a tic, I will have the Sergeant drive you over in your car."

"No you won't! I won't go. You haven't charged me with any crime."

"This is not the US. I needn't charge you at this time. And you will go, even if I have to clap you in irons." Now be still." At this he beckoned the Sergeant who came at a trot. After explaining his new duties to the Sergeant, the Inspector returned to his car. The driver quickly let him in and they drove off.

"I am sorry miss. He is altogether mad at the moment. I don't know at all what has come over him. Will we go now, please? It's best if we don't keep him waiting, with him on a tear and all."

"Of course Sergeant. I suppose it is best to not irritate him further. God forbid that I should irritate him further. I am so confused. Should I get a lawyer? I mean a Solicitor? Is he going to charge me?

"It is not my place to advise you miss. However you can be sure that I will let Liam know what has happened, and I am sure that he will be in to you in a flash. No doubt he will also let the Murphy's know of your predicament. Not to tell you your business, but if you were to be very tired with it all when you get to the station, you might be able to rest for a while."

"Thank you Sergeant." I am amazed at the genuine kindness I found in most people in Ireland. They seem to take a genuine interest in your welfare. I am sure that the Sergeant was sticking his neck out. Not that I would ever tell anyone, but he couldn't be sure of that. We rode silently into Mallow, and soon arrived at the station. I could see that the Superintendent had already arrived. No doubt poised to pounce upon my arrival. I had been thinking of how to handle him while we drove over. It seemed that if I was very contrite and feigned cooperation, I could stall the interview until the Sergeant could get hold of Liam and the Murphy's. I couldn't think of anything else to do anyway.

I was right about the Superintendent being ready to pounce. No sooner had we walked through the front door than he appeared at my side grasping my elbow once again. "Now, will we continue where we left off." This opening was said in a very gruff voice. No doubt to let me know who was in control of the situation.

"Superintendent, could I say something before we start?"

"Of course Miss O'Donovan."

"I am very sorry for my behavior back at the house."

"Oh, well I...uh I can understand."

"No please let me go on Superintendent. There is no excuse for my behavior. You are only doing your job. I am afraid that I got terribly confused, what with my father's death, the break-in to my home and then finding a body on the trail. Not that any of this excuses my behavior, but I am sure you can understand why I am so distraught. I want nothing better than to get this all over with, the same as you." He looked at me with a puzzled expression on his face. I wonder if I could rest for a bit before we start, Superintendent?" I looked as contrite and tired as I could. "Also if it is not too much of a bother could I have a cup of tea?" He didn't look sold. Conflicting emotions ran across his face. In the end Irish courtesy won.

"You can of course. I'll have the Sergeant bring you a cup. He'll take you into a room where you can rest for a bit. When you feel a little better we can continue." I was surprised by the sincerity in his voice. Maybe I had misjudged him. In a few moments the Sergeant returned, cup of tea in hand and took me to a small room with a cot, a chair and a desk.

"Liam and the Murphy's will be here straight away miss." He then left me alone waiting in a small room in a police station in Mallow, County Cork, Ireland

CHAPTER FIFTEEN

I hadn't very long to wait. There were very loud voices in the corridor outside the room. There was a lot of running about outside the room. And soon there was a lot of coming in inside the room. Liam led the cortege with Patrick and Mrs. Murphy bringing up the rear. They all had long faces and apologetic demeanors about them. Though it was hard to see why. They certainly hadn't contributed to this mess, unless of course one of them had bumped off Donal. What a ridiculous idea, I was really letting things get to me. None of them would have any reason to kill Dad. Liam was the first to speak.

"I am so sorry, Colleen. I have no idea, well, no firm idea as to what the Superintendent is up to."

As he was speaking, Cliona came up to me and took my arm. She gently led me out of the room with the others tagging along behind. Patrick had said nothing. His expression had not changed a bit. God! I wonder if he thought I was guilty. He couldn't possibly. All of a sudden I was filled with a sort of dread. I wanted to hear him speak, to offer his condolences. Nothing, not a word left his mouth.

When we came to the front room of the station we

all stopped and Liam came alongside me. "If you will wait for us here please Colleen, Cliona and I'll see to the formalities, so." Cliona waltzed me over to a bench where I was sat. It felt like an off key dream; being led about with little or no will of my own, long faced Patrick looming over me as I sat as Madame Lafarge - no, not Madame Lafarge - I was not gleefully contemplating the misery of another, nor was I knitting. I still felt like her though.

In a minute Liam was back a grim look on his face. "We're set for now. That is a bloody minded bastard though." I suggest we all go to the hotel bar for a drink and we can talk this over."

"Splendid idea Liam," said Cliona. Liam nodded his assent. Liam abruptly hauled me to my feet, and we headed out the front door. We turned right and headed down the hill through an alley into town. On Main Street we turned left our spirits rising geometrically to the distance from the station. That is all spirits except Patrick, he seemed more morose than ever. I turned to him, "Patrick are you that unhappy to seem me released from the slammer?"

"What Colleen? Oh! No, no, not at all. I'm as delighted as the rest. It's just that I've been thinking of a line in your Dad's notes that is bothering me."

"My Dad's notes? How did you come by them?"

"When Liam called I checked for you next door. Silly I know, but just to make sure that it wasn't maybe someone else at the station. The papers were sitting on the table in the hall, and I can spare no unread piece of paper. Sorry, I know I was being nosy."

"I don't mind, Patrick." In fact I felt quite

relieved. Now that he was talking again he was his old self. I cared more than I wanted to admit. "But what did you see in the papers that I didn't?"

"It was just a short note. It probably means nothing, but it started me thinking. Can we wait till we're inside? I'll explain my thoughts then." We turned into the hotel, which looked very plain on the outside. There was a small reception area that looked quite elegant, considering it was in a market town, not a tourist center. We passed through and went into the bar in the back. It was beautiful. There was lots of dark wood and frosted glass. The bar was long with a brass footrail. It could have been a movie set. Cliona and I went to a table in an alcove, while Patrick and Liam went to the bar to get our drinks.

Liam turned back our way and half shouted, "What will you have Colleen?" As soon as he had said it Patrick grabbed his arm and said something to him. Whatever he said appeared to amuse Liam who glanced back at me and appeared to chuckle. I felt that this was all at my expense. Cliona must have sensed my discomfort. "Colleen, I think Liam is used to his women ordering a gin and tonic. We don't know many Americans. I think your father was the first American I really got to know."

"Its allright Cliona. Liam didn't hurt my feelings. I just didn't know what I had done that was amusing." In a minute the men came over with the drinks. "Sorry Colleen, I am just not used to women ordering whiskey"

"That's OK Liam. My father started me drinking with whiskey. I suppose its not all that usual back home either. Not unless its in a cocktail of some sort. Patrick can we hear what it is that has been bothering you?"

"Sure, there was a short note in the margin, "Check out the Super." That's all it said. I don't think I would have paid it any attention if the Superintendent had not taken you back to the station."

"I don't see what difference that makes Patrick. Him taking me to the station, I mean"

"Why did he do that? He couldn't think you a serious suspect. I just couldn't think of a valid reason for him to take you back for questioning."

"I was very testy with him when he first arrived at Donal's. I think he took me back to the station to teach me a lesson."

"That well may be, but what if he had a different reason. He was also very reluctant to release you until Liam pointed out how little evidence there was against you."

Patrick leaned over and assumed a conspirital attitude. His voice actually lowered a notch. "Now, I know this is a bit of a s-stretch, but it is plausible, or maybe I s-should say possible. Consider, we don't know who killed either Colleen's father or Donal Kelly. We can, however, for the sake of argument, assume it was the same person. Why was your father killed Colleen? Let us assume he knew s-something damaging about the S-Superintendent. S-suppose also that the S-Superintendent found out and met your father to confront him. They fought and your father was killed. Remembering the note in the margin started my train of thought."

"I think your train is off the tracks, Patrick," said Liam.

"Yes it might well be. However let me f-f-finish."

"Patrick you're stuttering."

"Oh thanks mother. When I get excited, Colleen, my brain gets ahead of me and I start to stutter. Anyway the Superintendent then realizes that he needs a culprit, and he needs to find the information that your Dad had in his possession. Then Donal falls into his lap as the murderer. That solves his first problem. Next he breaks into your father's house to find whatever incriminating material your father has. He doesn't find what he's looking for and leaves. Later he finds out about the note in the margin from Liam. Did you tell him about that Liam?"

"I might have. I don't really remember though. I didn't pay much attention to that note. Not like you have done."

"Well, let's assume that you did tell him. He also knows since there was a confrontation that there is some damaging information. In fact, he wouldn't have to know about the note I guess." Everyone chuckled at this. Patrick seemed to be arguing with himself and losing but he went on. "So he has two problems, one, a culprit who appears to be guilty, but who he knows isn't, and two, missing incriminating information. If he can arrest and successfully try Donal he eliminates problem one, but Donal may, in the end, be able to prove his innocence. And he is still left with the second problem. I think he his now convinced that you Colleen have the information or soon will have. So he needs you out of the way, and how better than to have you arrested with all of your energy directed toward getting acquitted. I don't think he really had any hope of actually convicting you. You were a likely suspect for Donal's murder because of the bad feeling between he and your father, but probably not a reasonable enough suspect. In any case acting on this he arranged to have Donal killed, which he was, when fate threw you into his lap. He didn't expect to have you find Donal's body, but when you did, he acted, quickly."

"Well."

"Well."

"Well."

Three voices, one thought. We looked at one another not sure how to respond. Cliona looked slightly amused. Liam looked a bit irritated. I don't know how I looked, but I know how I felt. Crazy, but possible. It did explain the Superintendent's treatment of me since his arrival at the murder scene, but there were other equally plausible explanations. He may actually think me guilty, or he may have only resented the way I reacted to him. "Patrick, I think it is possible. I don't think it probable, though. What could a police officer in Ireland have done that would warrant murder. I guess I mean what could he have done that my father could have found out about?

"I don't know, Colleen. I think you will have to search the house again to see if you can find anything at all. I wonder, did your Dad send you anything while you were still in Oregon?"

"Just the normal letters and such. He never sent any notes, or anything other than the usual news. You know, I don't remember him ever mentioning the Superintendent. So the answer is no. He never sent me anything in Oregon. As far as searching the house, I'll do it again if you wish. Don't hold out much hope though. I did a pretty good job the first time."

All the time we were talking, Liam was getting more and more agitated. Finally he couldn't stand it any longer. "Will you ever leave off Patrick! I admit that the Superintendent is a queer enough fellow. But he is no more the murderer than is the ghost of Dromineen. Now I'll not go into the problems with your bit of a story. I think we have wasted enough time on this."

At this point Cliona chimed in. "Patrick, I do think Liam may be right."

Liam spoke gratefully, "Thank you Cliona. Patrick I apologize for taking your head off. It wasn't warranted. I must be a wee bit sensitive to criticism of the Garda. But, in the absence of any hard evidence I think our attention should be turned elsewhere."

Patrick's grin broke out. "I see I'm a majority of but one. I'll acquiesce, and your apology is accepted Liam. I think we should finish our drinks and get Colleen home so she can store up energy for tomorrow."

"What do I need energy for Patrick?"

"I think Patrick means for our trip to Dublin," said Cliona. It's not tomorrow Patrick. It's the day after. In any case, I hope you'll join Patrick and I. It'll get your mind off of all of this. While Patrick is whiling away his day in the library, you and I can do the shops proud."

"But it is tomorrow mother. You see I...oh yes, uh no it isn't tomorrow is it? Well then you have all the more time to store up your energy Colleen."

"That's worth storing up energy. I wouldn't miss Dublin for the world." And an extra day will help Patrick, thanks. But before we go I'm curious about something. Liam's comment reminded me that someone at Dad's funeral said that the murderer was the ghost of Dromineen. What did they mean?

"We have old records at the Gard station about

reports of the ghost. In fact I've met a sergeant who saw the ghost. One of his men shot at it."

"Liam that can't be. Surely the stories are no more than that?"

"I can't say that I believe them Colleen, but the record says that every seventeen years an apparition appears at Dromineen in the dead of the night. He is a comely gentleman carrying a lantern, and is dressed in Elizabethan finery. He beckons people towards himself and leads them to their death over the cliff into the river below."

"Didn't you threaten me with the ghost when I was little."

Of course not, Patrick. I would never use a ruse with my own child."

I could see that something had passed between Patrick and his mom. They both had a slightly bemused look on their faces. "What's going on with you two? You both look very pleased with yourselves."

"Nothing really Colleen. Its just that as a child Patrick would always blame the ghost of Dromineen whenever he was late and not of a mind to explain the cause of the delay."

We all laughed, drained our drinks and left.

CHAPTER SIXTEEN

I had slept all right and was grateful for a day with nothing to do. I could call Portland and see if Dad had done anything about the Superintendent. His note in the margin could have meant anything, but it wouldn't hurt to try. Patrick could be right. It was a pretty flimsy argument but I should check it out, if only for Patrick's sake.

I was getting hungry, and thought I'd better start wrestling the big stove in the kitchen. Cliona had one just like it. It was called an AGA, and, according to Cliona, it was always on. There were two large burners under the chrome lids. One was hot enough to boil, and the other was for simmering. It also had three ovens that were at different temperatures. What a gas. I found the oatmeal in the pantry, and a pan under the counter. I gingerly opened the large chrome lid to the boiling burner. It was very hot, and large, about the size of a cast-iron camping skillet. There seemed to be room for at least three pots on the burner. I suppose I shouldn't call it a burner. It looked like a large thick metal plate, kind of like where you put pots on an old wood stove. In any case the water was boiling immediately so I threw in the oatmeal and moved the pot to the other burner to simmer away.

While the porridge was cooking I went to dress. I decided to skip a shower or bath since I didn't want to fuss with the hot water. I dressed quickly and went into the den. Dad's address book was sitting on top of the desk along with the rest of the mess left from the search. "I wonder if I can direct dial?" I thought to myself. I quickly found a local phone book. Sure enough the directions were right in the front of the book. I put through the call, and waited for an answer. As I was waiting it occurred to me that it was just a little after midnight in Portland. I hung up quickly before I had to explain to anyone. Feeling a little foolish I went back into the kitchen.

The oatmeal was perfect. I served it up and sat at the kitchen table. I sat slowly eating and wondering what to do with my time. I would have to wait until three or so this afternoon before I called Lieutenant Novak. That would be about nine, back home. No, no wait, that would be only seven in Portland. He wouldn't be in for a couple more hours most likely. If Dad had made any inquiries about the Superintendent it would have been to Novak. They went way back so I had better wait until five before I called. I suppose I could spend some time straightening the mess in the house. I should also walk around the property. I had no idea what shape the yard was in. In fact I had no idea just how much property Dad had. That is what I would do. In fact I would do a little gardening if I could find tools.

I cleaned up my mess and went outside. I'd clean the house later. It was overcast with a small break in the clouds across the valley to the North. It could turn out to be a nice day, or it could rain, or both - a lot like Portland. I walked towards Cliona's house. There really wasn't anything but a gravel path between the two houses. The path had stepping-stones so I walked to the back of the house. In the back there was a high hedge between the two back yards. I walked closer to the hedge. I couldn't believe my eyes. The hedge was a fuscia. Actually it was probably many, many fuscias. I hadn't noticed the flowers until I was quite close. It was astounding. It was gorgeous. I couldn't take my eyes off it. I suppose I shouldn't have been so surprised. I had seen wild fuscia when I was driving here. Still the impact was amazing.

The hedge actually enclosed three sides of a very well kept back yard. This was amazing. I couldn't remember Dad ever doing any yard work at home. In his defense I have to admit that he probably didn't have the time. The grass looked like it could use mowing. If I could find a mower I'd do that. The flowerbeds looked fine, which was just as well since other than being able to tell a rose from just about any other flower was the extent of my horticultural abilities.

I walked around the back of the house and took a path that led by the other side of the house back to the front. About halfway along the wall there was a door. I opened the door and walked into a utility and storage room. There was a washer and dryer along one wall next to a utility sink. At one end of the room was another door that, I assume, went into the house, probably the kitchen. At the other end of the room was a lawn mower, as well as lot of other tools and supplies. Was I really going to do this? Sure I was. I grabbed the mower and hefted it outside. It was really old, but looked like it had been well cared for. There was a basket attached so I wouldn't have to rake the grass when I was done.

It was very pleasant walking that mower across the grass. The first time the basket filled I had a hard time finding out where to dump the clippings. I finally found a break in the hedge that led to the pasture behind the house. From the pile of old clippings and lawn debris I quickly deduced that this is where the clippings should be dumped. I don't suppose it should have taken even an hour to mow the yard, but I was daydreaming as I pushed the mower around so it took twice as long. The clouds had broken and it was getting warmer which slowed me even more. Finally I was done. I dumped the last load of clippings and took the mower back to the utility room. When I put the mower away I saw a pair of edging scissors. It was so nice and peaceful outside. I hadn't thought about Dad or anything else. I grabbed the scissors and went back outside.

It didn't work as well this time. Somehow what Patrick had said about the Superintendent began to make sense. I really don't think it began to make sense as much as I just couldn't get it out of my head, but I told myself that it really made sense. Cutting away at the grass wasn't the therapy that mowing had been. I started to get really angry even though I couldn't think of any reason why the Superintendent would have killed Dad. And the nerve of the man to haul me into jail for no reason whatsoever, just to cover his own tracks. I didn't notice how furiously I was cutting away at the lawn until I almost cut off my thumb. I had hacked away without paying attention. What had been a very straight line had become quite a gouge into the lawn. I felt a little foolish.

It was ridiculous getting this worked up when I hadn't checked with Portland yet. I decided to quit tearing up the yard. Maybe a walk up the hill would calm me down.

After putting everything away I went into the house. Sure enough the door at the back of the utility room led into the kitchen. I wondered why I hadn't seen it before, or maybe I had and just forgot. I grabbed a jacket and went back out the back door. I went through the break in the hedge and started climbing up the pasture in back of the houses. The weather had cleared a little causing the sun to sweep across the pasture ahead of me as each break in the clouds arrived and then moved on. The hill was steep and I soon had to slow down. There weren't any cows that I could see. I wouldn't have a repeat of the chase across from Dromineen Castle. I climbed on. Finally I got tired enough that I had to stop to rest. The sun was appearing regularly making it to hot to wear my jacket. I took it off and plopped myself down.

I had climbed quite a way up. I impressed myself, wow. The house was well below me hung just above the village further down. I could see sparkles of the river through the trees that lined its banks way off in the distance. The few cars that were traveling along the Killarney road looked like toys. The great houses that lined the hills across were elegant in their mannered placement along the crest of the valley. A rabbit broke from the hedgerow on my left running from an imagined fox, or at least a very lazy fox. He turned on a dime and sped back into the hedge not twenty feet from where he started. This, I suppose, is how I had imagined Ireland would be not that I really thought of Ireland very much. I never really expected to be here. Dad's move had seemed strange to me at the time. I had thought him a bit silly, although romantic, when he had told me he was coming here. I still don't know why he came, but after meeting Cliona, and Patrick, and all, I could see why he stayed.

I must have sat for over half an hour taking in the view. I debated whether I should get back to the house or finish climbing to the top of the pasture. I was well over half way there. I jumped up filled with resolve. Trudging upward I wondered what Dublin might be like. I had only seen pictures of O'Connell Street and the bridge over the Liffey. No, no, I had a poster of those great doors too. Well I was looking forward to the trip. "Onward Christian Soldiers marching as..." I couldn't remember any more of the words, but those kept running through my head as I pressed on to the top of the pasture.

Finally I reached the end. I was high enough that the house looked more like a dollhouse than something real. I watched as a car came up the road from the village. I thought of a train set that had been set up in the window of a Department Store for Christmas. The car looked so small. It turned into the shared drive between Cliona's and Dad's. Someone got out. I couldn't tell who it was. It was too far away. They walked over to my door, not Cliona's. It had to be important. I was sure of it. I started to run back, and quickly decided that I had better slow down or I would end up rolling all the way back. Before long I was half way down. I could see that whoever it was had given up knocking at the door as was starting to leave. I shouted, but I don't think they heard, so I started going faster, and sure enough I fell and began rolling. I stopped myself finally and got up covered with grass and a few other items I wasn't overly pleased to have plastered on my body. I must have made quite a commotion, because whoever it was that had been calling had come round to the back and was watching my antics with apparent delight.

As I got closer I could see that it was Liam to whom I was providing such grand entertainment. He certainly seemed to be enjoying it all. "Have you come with some news about my Father, or are you here simply to make fun of me."

"Oh no, no, no, not at all. But aren't you no more than playing Maureen O'Hara's part in "The Quiet Man" as John Wayne is finally facing up to the brother. You know, where he is dragging her through the fields, the whole village following in anticipation of the fight to come."

"You keep on like this and I'll show you a fight."

"I'll bet you would, but I actually came to ask you to dinner, not to start a fight."

"Dinner? You want to ask me to dinner?" I couldn't believe it. Liam was a very good-looking man, but I had thought he was Patrick's best friend. I thought I'd let the two of them worry about that though. A dinner out sounded very tempting, and he should be good company, particularly if I could get him to stop laughing at me. "Where would we go. I mean, I don't know Liam. I barely know you."

"Of course you barely know me. You barely know anyone here, and what better chance to get to know someone than over a good meal."

"I would enjoy getting away from the house, I'll have to admit. What time would you like to go?"

"Will I fetch you at eight?"

"Yes, that would be very nice. Where are we going?"

"I think Longueville House. William O'Callaghan the son of the owners is one of Ireland's best chefs. It is an elegant cut stone Georgian Manor Home that you will enjoy seeing."

"What will I wear? I don't have anything for such a fancy place. Do I need to buy an evening gown or cocktail dress?"

"Not at all, at all. Any regular dress will do quite well indeed. It's not formal. I have only seen people dressed formally during race week many years ago. So, you needn't worry in the least. I'll pick you up at eight." With a brief wave as he turned and walked to his car, Liam left me to my own devices. As I walked into the house I suddenly felt very tired. I had been on the hill for quite a while, but I couldn't believe it when I looked at the clock. It was after three. Still too early to call Portland. I was a little hungry, but thought that I should save my appetite for tonight. So, I decided to take a nap

CHAPTER SEVENTEEN

I woke confused, not knowing where I was. The room was strange. The bed was strange. The floor was strange. I struggled to sit up. The covers were all twisted about me. Dad's cottage, Ireland, that's where I am. Boy that climb up the hill must have really taken it out of me. I couldn't even remember coming into the room to lie down. I looked at the clock on the dresser. It was after six. I'd slept for three hours. I stood up and walked into the bathroom to splash myself awake. I hadn't dreamt at all. Liam had been very polite. No, not polite, very, I don't know, accomodating? Not that either. In any case I was looking forward to tonight.

The kitchen was a mess from this morning. I hadn't cleaned a thing. Quickly I began cleaning the dishes I had used earlier. Just as I was about done I remembered that I should call Portland. It should be morning there. Novak could be at his desk. I stopped cleaning, wiped my hands on a towel, and went into the den. I had written the number on a piece of paper and tucked it under the phone. I dialed, waited a few rings, and Maisy answered. "Lieutenant Novak's desk." "Maisy, this is Colleen O'Donovan calling from Ireland.

Is Novak around there anywhere?"

"Colleen how nice to hear from you. I was so sorry to hear about your Dad. It really shook us all up."

"Thanks Maisy. This might have something to do with Dad. I need to see if he called or wrote Novak about a Superintendent Mundell."

"Novak's not here Colleen. He's out on a case. I don't think he'll be back today. I can have the dispatcher give him a message."

"No I don't think that's necessary. Just have him call me here at Dads' when he gets back in. If I'm not here there is an answering machine. He can just leave a message."

"I'll tell him Colleen. By the way I do kind of remember your Dad calling about a month ago asking Novak to look up something about somebody in Ireland. The name could have been Mundell"

"Oh that could be it Maisy. Be sure and have Novak call me. Do you remember what Dad wanted to know?"

"No I really don't. I don't even know if Novak found out anything, and I can't remember who it was. Anyway I'll have him call.

"Thanks Maisy," I hung up wondering if there could be anything to Patrick's suspicions. Liam wouldn't be happy, but I thought I wouldn't bring it up until I heard from Novak. No need to spoil the evening. I had a hard time not walking over to Cliona's to tell Patrick, but there wasn't really anything to tell him yet. So I started to get ready for my evening with Liam.

While I was getting all gussied up I couldn't help

comparing the two men. Patrick was very kind, not really good looking, but quite attractive in a rumpled sort of way. Liam was very good looking, and I think the sort of man that as a young girl I had been told to avoid. And the sort of man I never could avoid. Not that I knew him very well, but I would have to be on my toes tonight. What a lovely thought.

As I was finishing I heard Liam drive up. I adjusted the only dress that I had brought with me and walked to the front door. Before I got there Liam knocked. I quickly opened the door. I really was anticipating a good time. A good time, who was I kidding, I was expecting a great time. "Hello Colleen," he said. "Ah but your lookin lovely tonight."

"Thanks Liam. It's all I have to wear. I hope it's OK for tonight."

"Ah sure and won't you be the bell of the ball. Now if you'll accompany me to me chariot we'll be off."

Liam led me by the arm to his car. He opened the door for me and I got in. Liam's car was quite a bit larger than Patrick's. I couldn't tell what kind it was, but it was very comfortable, and as I was to quickly find out, it was also very fast. As soon as we left the house we sped down the hill into and through the village. We went back the same way that I had traveled before, but at a pace that left me breathless. I couldn't even complain to Liam for fear of taking his attention away from driving. One good thing about his speed, we were out on the main road where I stopped to look at the castle before I had time to get really scared.

He turned right off the main road just after he got

to where I had stopped. We went along no more than a few hundred yards when we came to a giant gate. The pillars were cut stone at least ten feet high. Two giant halves of a black wrought iron gate hung from each. They were thrown open welcoming us up the gravel drive. We passed a small gatekeeper's cottage with three or four cars parked around it. The cottage was also cut stone. It was perched on the bank of a small stream with a cut stone bridge. We crossed the bridge and started up a hill. On our left was a wood, and on the right pasture with ambling sheep. The gravel drive wound up the hill beyond the wood until we were high above pasture on the left. Rhododendrons were massed on the right now. As we turned a bend in the road a magnificent mansion came into view. The magnificence of the sight took my breath away. It was like being startled, but pleasant. Liam drove to the front step, a portico with columns and the roof of a Greek Temple.

We walked up to a giant door. I expected a Major Domo to open the door and greet us. Liam simply opened the door and we walked in. The hall was a little strange. It was floored with Portland Stone. A very thin rug was centered in the hall beneath a very ornate chandelier. Immediately below the chandelier was a four-part settee that looked like it was made for a New Orleans Bordello. Liam turned left and went into a small room that must have been the bar.

"What'll you have pet? Go into the drawing room now, and I'll bring in the drinks."

"A whiskey please." Pet? I was his pet? Not for a minute. I was no man's pet for crying out loud. Was this evening going to be more work than it was worth? I was beginning to wonder. Well he'd soon find out that he did not have a pushover on his hands. If that is what he had in mind. I walked through the bar into the drawing room. It was very elegant. In the center of the wall away from the windows was a gigantic fireplace. A very welcoming fire burned away. A group of chairs and a couch were arranged around the fireplace forming a "U." Behind this there were chairs and tables grouped at each window. The effect was many intimate places where people could talk to one another, or to other groups. I had felt somewhat overwhelmed by Longueville until I came into this room. It was very elegant, but it also was closely personal and welcoming.

I sat in a chair by the window, and waited for Liam to bring the drinks. Looking out I could see the castle at the foot of the property. There were sheep in the meadow that was right in front of the house. This meadow was sloped down to another field at the bottom of the hill where more sheep grazed. I sat a little mesmerized with the view until Liam came with the drinks. He had a strange look on his face as I looked up. It left him as soon as he saw my gaze. He smiled a wan smile, handed me my drink, and sat down. "I find it one of the finest views in Ireland, Colleen. These people, the O'Callaghans have taken an old wreck of a house and built it into one of the finest Country Manor homes in all of Ireland. Their oldest son, William, is a very fine chef. You'll not find better in Europe, and his wife, Aisling, is a marvelous hostess. Her Granda was my Da's boss in the Gard. Old man Kelly was quite a character, he was. A fine man indeed. Have you ever heard of the ghost of Dromineen?"

"Yes, I have. Someone suggested that my father was most likely killed by the ghost."

"That may seem more than a little fanciful, but the ghost is taken quite seriously by more than one person. When Kelly was the sergeant of the Gard he was out at night with two men. They were setting an ambush for a poteen maker when..."

"A poteen maker? What's a poteen maker?"

"Poteen is moonshine, illegal whiskey - deadly stuff. Unfortunately it's still widely available. Anyway, one of the men saw a light by the castle. They were hidden in the bushes close by. Having heard that poteen was to be sold that night at the castle. They all crept forward very careful, being sure that what they were seeing was the lantern of the poteen maker. When they had crept next to the main house they got a fierce fright. The lantern was being held by an apparition. It appeared to be an Elizabethan Gentleman dressed in the finery of the time. He was holding a lantern aloft, and beckoned to them. One of the men fired his carbine and the apparition disappeared only to reappear at the far end of the house, again beckoning to them. The man that had fired the shot raced over to the figure, which now was moving through the window and suspended over the river below. Sergeant Kelly and the other man caught the first fellow just in time to prevent him from plummeting to the river."

"Liam, you can't possibly believe any of this."
"I suppose I don't, really, but wait there's more. In 1957, I think, or about then, a child was missing. The Gard had looked everywhere. Finally they got a garbled story from another boy who had been playing with the fellow that was missing. It seems they were on the doss that day."

"On the what?"

"On the doss. Staying out of school, you know."

"OK, go on."

"As the day went on they became more and more afraid of going home for fear of reprisal from their parents, as you can well imagine. Anyway it became dark it seems while they were still at the castle. Now the story becomes quite garbled at this point, but the Gard thinks this is what happened. The boys were close to the house when they saw the same apparition. You have to remember the story of the ghost of Dromineen was common in this area. The missing boy went to investigate, and the other fellow fled in abject terror. Well now the Gard were neither believing or not believing the ghost bit, but felt that the story at least located where they might continue their search for the missing lad. Early the next morning the Gard all turned out at the foot of the castle. By noon of that day not only had they found the remains of the missing boy, but they removed six other bodies from the mud of the river. Apparently they were fairly well preserved having been buried in the mud. A lot of the clothing was still on the bodies. According to reports published at the time the clothes indicated that these people had been falling in there about twice a century for the last three hundred years. Well as you can imagine the Ghost of Dromineen gained great credence as a result."

"Sure Liam, sure he did."

"I know it is a bit of stretch, but it is hard to argue with each of the bodies being dressed in clothes of the various periods, and them going back three hundred years. Having said that, I suspect the area has been used for smuggling for centuries. Most likely the truth is that the bodies are those of various villains that met their end when they were up to no good. And the castle itself was used to billet troops right after the confiscation."

"Were there really smugglers there, Liam?"

"Oh yes. It is a dark and mostly deserted place. The ghost keeps people away, and there are rumors of caves in the area, although no one seems to know where they might be."

I started at his comment about the caves. I don't think he noticed at all. I didn't really want to tell him about my discovery for some reason. I looked up to make some interested sort of comment when I noticed a tall young woman standing behind Liam.

"Will I take your order?" As she said this she gave me a little wink. I wondered what she meant by that. Colleen are you ready to order?"

"I am Liam, but could you order for me. I don't see a single thing on the menu that I wouldn't like, and I'm sure you're quite familiar with what they serve here."

"I'll do that, of course. Now, I'll start with the terrine of oxtail with foie gras, gribiche sauce and garden salad. Colleen will start with the chicken and crab sausage on wild rice with the light curry. For the second course we'll both have the seafood bisque, and keeping up the tradition here we'll both have the monkfish medallions with the basil couscous, saffron and orange sauce. I think we'll attend to desert after dinner. Is that all right with you Colleen?"

"Oh Liam it sounds delicious, thanks." Liam then ordered a bottle of white wine - Chateau de Chasagne, a Montrachet. We sat talking about nothing really until we had finished our drinks. A short time later the young woman who had taken our order came over and asked us if we were ready to go over. I wasn't sure what she meant, but I thought she was asking us to go into the dining room, which she was. We walked through a room about the same size as the bar. The sidewalls were lined with bookcases. There was a small fireplace blazing away at the back. There were four empty tables set for dinner. "This room's for the smokers," Liam said. We went through another door and walked into the main dining room. The woman sat us in the back corner and seated me looking out into the room.

"You look very lovely this evening, you know."

"Why thank you Liam. I think I can truthfully say, Oh this old thing. It really is old, but the best I have to offer at this point in time. My god Liam, you're blushing. Whatever for?"

"I don't know, I just that, well I... hmm. I can't remember blushing since I was a young child. It makes no sense whatsoever." Just then the young woman returned with our first course. Liam quickly set about eating. Quite relieved at not having to explain himself further. I really was confused. I hadn't said anything that could be considered provocative or suggestive, and I had no intention of doing so. Not knowing what else to do at this moment, I followed Liam's example and began eating. I had never had a sausage with such smooth consistency. The sausage itself was relatively mild, mostly the flavor of the crab and the chicken with only a hint of garlic. But the curry was like no other that I had ever tasted. It had the musky taste of a traditional Indian curry but added a piquancy that set off the flavors of the sausage. There was no where near enough. A first course should leave you hungry, ready for more. This had most certainly had succeeded. No sooner had we finished the first course than the second arrived. We hadn't spoken a word. The bisque was fresh with a subtle combination of tomato and seafood. While it was filling it did not dazzle, as had the first course. Finally we both finished that course, and sat back.

"Now, Colleen, wasn't that very good indeed?"

"It was very good Liam. If the main course is anything like it this could turn out to be the best meal I've ever had."

"I'm very glad to hear it." "Liam, you're avoiding the subject."

"Expertly in fact. If I do say so myself."

"Avoid it no more. Why did you blush?"

"Could I ask a great favor? When we have finished the meal I'll be more than happy to explain. I fear it might lessen the pleasure of our dinner. Would you please indulge me?"

"This is all very mysterious, but yes, I'll indulge you. What could be so serious? Well never mind. I see our waitress approaching." For the rest of the meal all of our conversation was small talk. I know that Liam wanted to say more, but was afraid now, afraid of offending maybe. I don't know. It was strange. The meal, however, continued to be better with every course. The waitress placed the dish in front of me. The center of the plate contained a timbale of couscous. Around that mound the monkfish medallions were carefully arranged. Each of the medallions was gently browned. All of this sat in a pool of orange and saffron sauce. I was reluctant to start. The presentation was as good as I have ever seen. But, I couldn't resist the smells that rose off the plate. Cautiously I placed my fork along the center of one of the monkfish medallions. Gently I pushed until it split in half and slid into some of the couscous. Slowly I placed it in my mouth. The flavor was very strange. Like the starter, musky, because of the saffron, but bright from the orange. When this was combined with the solid flesh of the monkfish, and the graininess of the couscous it was heaven. Quickly I glanced at Liam. Could he possibly have known how superbly the courses that I had chosen would complement each other. After all he had completed the order after I made the initial choice. I was impressed

I couldn't remember enjoying food quite as much as I did that night. Finally we finished. I looked at Liam expectantly, not saying a word, just waiting. He smiled. Not a pleasant smile. Not that it was mean or nasty. No just that I think he didn't really want to say what he knew he had to say.

"This has become very difficult for me Colleen. Now, I'm not trying to get out of it. It's just that I wish that I could. You wouldn't want to just forget it all now would you?"

"I don't think so Liam. Carry on."

"Shit, I was afraid that you would say that. Well then, It would seem that I... You sure you want to hear this? I most certainly don't want to say it,"

"Carry on Liam. You started this."

Yes, well. It, it, it, now don't be angry, please. I have reserved a room for the night for us, and I wondered, well actually I don't wonder at all now. Please excuse me, I know it was a very stupid thing to do. It's just that I find you very attractive and I... Oh dear. Judging from the look on your face I am not forgiven."

"You sure as hell are not. Liam how could you. This would have been a perfect evening. I think I want to go home. Oh how could you. I just lost my father. I've only been her a few days. I've just met you, God." The man at the next table had a knowing smile on his face. His wife was looking at Liam with daggers. I turned to the man. "Why in hell don't you just mind your own fucking business." Well it seems that Liam was not the only person the blush that night. His wife gave me a smile, and a nod. The waitress, who had been hovering in the background, retreated. All of a sudden I understood her wink. It really pissed me off. I stormed out to the front porch and waited. Liam followed not saying a word. He brought the car around and we drove home without a word being spoken.

When we got to my house Liam ran around the car and opened the door. "Colleen is there anything I can say?"

"Liam it caught me by surprise. Don't be overly concerned. You did nothing sneaky or underhanded. In fact, if the truth were known I'm flattered, but at the same time it was rather insensitive. Don't worry about it. I'm sure we are still friends." I could see he was greatly relieved. I was glad I'd said that. I really didn't hold it against him. And he was certainly someone who I would expect it from. In any case he walked me to the door, and I dashed inside before anything more could happen.

CHAPTER EIGHTEEN

I had gone to bed as soon as I had come home. My night's sleep had been lousy. Strange dreams that I could almost remember had wakened me many times. Once, I got up with a feeling of great purpose, but had no idea what that purpose might be. The bed was a warm, comforting mess. I knew I had to get up to get ready to go to Dublin. Cliona had said that the train left Mallow at 10:20 AM. A neighbor was driving us over, so I had to be ready at 10:00 AM. I glanced at the clock. It was almost nine.

I got out of bed. I wrapped a blanket around myself. The cold of the room would raise goosebumps on a turtle. In the bathroom I turned on the water. While I was waiting for the water to get warm I ran back to the bedroom to get my clothes. When I got back, the water still was not warm. That was strange. It had run quite awhile. I kept testing the water getting more impatient each time I tested it. Obviously it was not going to warm up. After a moments thought, I went into the kitchen to warm enough water to take a sitzbath.

I was more than a little disappointed. A long warm shower would have been nice, but this would be OK. I splashed what little hot water there was in the most obvious places, scrubbed them thoroughly, and dried. As I was dressing, I wondered if my wool pantsuit would be all right for Dublin. The outfit was tailored and showed off my height well. The pants were herringbone tweed, the jacket a simple dark gray blazer. I had chosen an ivory blouse with a high lace collar. It was all very proper and smart. Very elegant, I thought to myself as I took a last glance in the mirror. I finished packing my suitcase, and went into the living room.

My coat was draped over the couch in the living room. No, no, it's called the sitting room. I should try harder to remember these things. Anyway, I picked up my coat, left the house, turned, and carefully locked the door. I didn't want to come back to find that the house had been ransacked again. I hoped I wasn't too early. My god, I'd forgotten to eat breakfast. Hopefully they would have food on the train.

When I got to the door it opened as I raised my hand to knock. "Good morning Colleen," said Patrick. "I was just coming to get you. We've been keeping breakfast for you." His grin was infectious. I could feel my face breaking into an unwanted smile. I was not a cheerful riser, and resented, a little, this intrusion into my grumpiness. But it was too late. My smile was there, not to be withdrawn.

"Patrick, you shouldn't have." It was out before I could stop it. I hated saying that. "Actually I'm glad you did. I skipped breakfast, and could use something to eat."

"Come in then, you're very welcome. Mother is in the kitchen waiting."

"Thanks," I replied as I went into the house.

"Good morning Colleen. Your outfit looks very Irish, quite right for Dublin," greeted Cliona as I walked into the kitchen. I must have been very apprehensive about my outfit. I could feel myself relax as soon as Cliona reassured me. And she did reassure me. Somehow she knew that I was concerned about how I looked, and kindly set my mind at ease. This was going to be a great day. I could feel it.

Cliona had prepared a delightful breakfast. She had bowls of fruit to put on the cereal, a basket of scones and muffins, and not a piece of bacon in sight. In the center of the table was a large bowl of oatmeal. Everything looked so good; I didn't know where to start. But start I did. "Cliona this is great. I can't remember when I've seen such a welcoming table."

"Thank you Colleen. It's very simple really. The scones and oatmeal only take a minute to make, and Patrick does the oatmeal. I don't bother when it is just me. Everything else is just bought at the market. You know, your Dad was always pleased to have breakfast here. He seemed to think it was something special. I never asked him, but always wondered what breakfast at home was like?"

"Not like this. It was every man for himself. In fact most all of our meals were. We just plopped whatever we needed on the table and ate. Seldom did we set the table like this. I wish we had, now. Maybe we would have spent more time together." All of a sudden I could feel my eyes tearing up. I was getting embarrassed with all this crying. Both Cliona and Patrick had, very politely, looked away. I concentrated on eating, and soon recovered. Unfortunately I had put a damper on the conversation at the table leaving us all to eat in silence. We had just about finished when the back door opened and a head stuck itself in declaring, "It's only Sonia." The rest of the person came in greatly pleased with herself, as apparently was Cliona.

"Its only Mary Igoe, Colleen. She and Mom have this thing from a TV show that for some strange reason provides them with unlimited amusement."

"Don't be stuffy Patrick. Colleen I'd like you to meet Mary. She's a neighbor on the other side from your father. She's being a dear and driving us to the station in Mallow."

"So, you're Mr. O'Donovon's daughter. We're so sorry for your troubles dear. If there is anything I can do to help, please just ask. As she was talking this short somewhat rough looking woman took my hands in hers. Somehow I could feel her sincerity and goodness through our clasped hands. I couldn't help returning her warm smile.

"I am very pleased to meet you Mrs. Igoe. You are very kind to offer your help and take us to the train."

"Not at all. I'm only going to market after, so. We'd best be leaving, though. The train's been on time of late."

"Do I have time to clean up here."

"No. Leave it. I'll straighten up when I'm back from Mallow."

We all left the table gathered our coats and suitcases and followed Mary out to her car. It was thankfully a little larger than Patrick's. Somehow we managed to all get in and store our suitcases. Cliona and I were jammed into the back with Patrick, knees to chin, was in the front passenger seat. Mary had a little trouble getting the car started, but soon we were once again returning to Mallow. The scenery on the route was becoming familiar. Somehow this pleased me, recognizing scenery in Ireland. Kind of like recognizing a scene in a movie.

We reached the roundabout in Mallow and went North out of the circle. We immediately turned right up the hill. When we got to the station I could see why Cliona wanted us to be driven to the station. There was a small parking lot to the right of the station. Every possible parking space and many impossible parking spaces had been taken. Many other people had the same idea we did, and the cars were lined up to drop them off. As we were getting out of the car the train pulled into the station. I got a little excited since I didn't have a ticket and didn't know if we were going to have enough time to buy tickets.

"Cliona, I don't have a ticket. Do we need to run so I can buy one and still catch the train?"

"Not at all Colleen. I have tickets for us all. The train won't leave for about ten minutes, so we have time enough to board."

I gathered my suitcase and followed into the station. As I entered the station I left it. There was an arch that I passed through that led to the train platform. The platform was covered, and there were two sets of tracks. The train was next to a platform on the other side of the tracks. The station building was very narrow and formed both sides of the arch. There were offices, restrooms, a small waiting room that did not appear to have ever been used, and a ticket window. To get to the other side we had to climb up a set of stairs that led to a covered overpass, cross over, and then go back down stairs. Once down Patrick led us to a non-smoking car. We stowed our luggage in a closet next to the bathroom and sat down. Cliona and I sat next to each other facing Patrick. There was a table between us. The train was very clean but worn. Probably it was well used. It didn't take long for most of the seats to fill up. Soon after there was an announcement from a formless person that the doors were about to close, and to please stand clear. They did. We were off to Dublin.

As the train pulled out of the station the same formless soul announced that this train was bound for Limerick Junction, Thurles, Portaloise, and Dublin. I felt like a world traveler. These strange romantic names. It may not be the Simplon Orient Express, but it was probably as close to it as I would ever get. We started high above the town as we left the station, but soon the ground caught up to us. We wound past the ruins of an old Abbey and soon were zipping along, slightly above the fields on both sides. Cliona and I were facing backwards which gave us a better view. You could watch something interesting longer since it took a long time to disappear from view going away from it.

Patrick was facing ahead, but it made little difference. As soon as we sat down he pulled out a pile of papers, spread them over the table and began writing furiously. Cliona was watching me watch Patrick. She had a wry smile on her lips. "We might as well sit back and enjoy the scenery, Colleen. When Patrick gets like this he's lost to the world."

"But he'll miss all this beautiful scenery."

"He's seen it many times, and I don't think scenery is very important to Patrick."

"Oh, I'll just watch it zoom on by then." I settled back in my seat next to the window. The train was moving quickly through the countryside. One farm after another zipped by. They were small, and all seemed to be dairy farms. I didn't see any crops. The sound of the train was becoming hypnotic. I could feel myself getting sleepier, and sleepier. Just as I was about to drop off we began to slow down. Soon we were in a station. The voice announced that we had arrived in Charleville. We traded some people in the train for some people on the platform, and started up again.

A pattern had started. Fields with men, their collies, and cows receding in the distance, Patrick writing away, me falling asleep, almost, pull into a station, exchange people, leave. After the fourth or fifth time I decided I would get up and stretch. "Cliona could you excuse me. I want to walk around for a bit."

"I can of course. Why don't I join you? We could go back to the dining car and have a bite to eat. The food is actually quite edible."

"I'd like that. I've never eaten on a train. In fact I haven't been on a train since I was a little girl. It's exciting." We walked back through three cars. Each was as full as ours. Finally we came to the dining car. It was like a long narrow school cafeteria. The tables were molded plastic with four plastic seats at each. In the back corner of the car a service area was tucked. It had cafeteria style rails to slide the trays along. It opened in two places. One, the smaller, faced the dining car. It looked like it was a bar. The other opening had the rails for the trays. There was a man behind each window.

"Sit here," said Cliona. We sat at the only empty table. "We can order from this breakfast menu. They'll bring it to us, or we can go to the window and have a sandwich or a snack if you don't want a cooked meal. They do a very nice salmon. See, it's at the bottom of the page. Look, there"

"I see it, thanks. It does look good. I'm not very hungry after that breakfast, but I do love salmon."

"You should have it then, It's only a small portion."

We both ordered the salmon, which was brought soon after we had placed our order. It was actually served on a china plate. There was potatoes, sliced green beans, and a small salad. The salmon was cooked properly. It was very moist, but not at all raw, really a very nice lunch. We didn't talk much while we were eating. Apparently travel had made us hungry. "Should we take something back for Patrick, Cliona?"

"No. He never eats on the train. There is a drinks trolley that goes up and down the aisles. So he can order coffee whenever he likes. Would you like to go back and see first class?"

"Is it real elegant with fancy windows and curtains?"

"No, not really. It is nicer than where we're sitting. The seats are larger and fancier, and there is more room. There is a station at each table where you can plug in a computer. But it isn't what I expected for the price they want."

"Why don't we just go back to our own seats then."

"OK"

We wound our way back through the cars. Kids were everywhere. No, not everywhere. They weren't in their seats. They were in the aisles having a great time. We came to our car, which didn't have many kids. Patrick was still working away, apparently oblivious to our departure. After I sat down I started to nod off. My head would slowly drop then straighten with a jerk. Finally someone's hand gripped my arm. I looked up. It was Cliona. Both she and Patrick were smiling at me. "Colleen, wake up, we're in Dublin." I heard someone saying that. It brought me full awake. I felt really excited. I must have been really looking forward to this trip. Dublin! I couldn't believe I was in Dublin.

CHAPTER 19

The Vicar frantically paced the hall. He was mumbling to himself all the while. Many times he turned to the Bishop's door, but always failed to go in. "They cannot summons me in this manner." He said under his breath. "Have they no idea who I am? This is intolerable, keeping me waiting in the hall like an errant schoolboy! They can't possibly know anything, not really. I have been most careful. And it is mine in any case. I have always replaced it in the past. It's just that I cannot go back for a while, not now." His self-righteous speech calmed him a bit. His pacing slowed, and some element of composure returned.

Eventually he calmed himself enough to sit in one of the chairs that lined the hall on either side of the Bishop's door. He sat in the chair closest to the door, but could only hear the murmur of voices inside. He strained to hear. It was to no avail. Resigned for the moment he began to study the chairs. The wood was very dark, almost black. They had to be very old. The legs of each chair continued up beyond the seat to form the arms and the back of the chair. They almost looked Roman. The arms and backs were finely carved. He wondered why he had not noticed them on previous visits. As he was looking at the chairs, his hand was gently rubbing the arm of his own chair. He looked at the arm where his hand was rubbing. It was rubbing a body, a twisted tormented body, carved in high relief in the arm of the chair. He hastily looked around at the other chairs. They were also carved in the same fashion. As he looked closer he realized that each chair was carved to represent one of the seven deadly sins. His chair was murder.

"This will not do," he muttered as he jumped up out of the chair. He turned to stare at the chair when the door opened. David stood in the doorway looking at the Vicar with a searching gaze. "Come in please, Vicar," David invited. "Sorry to have kept you waiting."

"That's quite all right," said the Vicar, obviously still shaken. They walked into the Bishop's study together. David motioned the Vicar to take a seat in front of the empty desk. "The Bishop will return in a moment," David explained as he took a seat behind the Vicar. No sooner had he made the statement than the Bishop walked in. His usual smile was missing as he sat without greeting the Vicar. He pulled a portfolio out of a drawer, placed it on his desk, opened it and began reading. After a moment he looked up and leaned forward towards the Vicar. "You sir, have been pilfering Church funds!"

The effect was like letting the air out of a balloon. The Vicar slumped in his chair. Both hands came up and cupped his face. He made a noise, an unidentifiable noise, the voice of despair. The Bishop and David sat and looked at him. They both were almost sorry for him, but not in the end. He began to speak, but they couldn't hear what it was that he was saying, it was so softly said. "I..I..I" the Vicar muttered then fell silent. Both men watched as he fought to gain control of himself. The Vicar's face began to relax. His breathing calmed. After a minute or so, he rose to his full height. "What sum of money do you find missing Bishop?"

The Bishop was somewhat taken aback. He had not expected such directness. Nevertheless he answered. "Thirteen Thousand punt, Vicar, is the amount that is missing."

"As much as that?" The Vicar began to lose his composure, but quickly reined it. He quickly turned and walked briskly to the door. As he left he turned and said. "You will have the money in full within a fortnight." With that he left.

The Bishop and David were both still rising when the Vicar left. "David, I am dumfounded. I did not expect that reaction. The man is far stronger than I ever imagined." Saying this the Bishop crashed back into his chair and chuckled. "I fear that I have once again underestimated that man. He did not even give me the opportunity to impose discipline. Which is just as well I am still unsure as to what course of action is best. By the way David, did your use of those chairs have any effect? He did seem unnerved when he came in."

"I think not Bishop. I was sure that he would sit on the side of the door where he could hear us. That's where I put Thieving. He was sittin on the other side. Something was bothering him when he entered, though. Probably it was just anticipation of your reaction to the embezzlement. He surely must have known he was caught when you summoned him after the audit?"

"That must be it David. I think I must remove him in the end. There are far too many complaints from his parishioners to leave him after this discovery. Did you sense that perhaps there is more to this than just stealing?"

"I don't know. He was acting strange before he came in. I could hear him pacing the hall. I just put that down to nervousness at being called here. I suppose one could imagine that his abrupt departure was to eliminate the possibility of being questioned further."

"He certainly could have. I fear, however, that we'll never know the complete truth. By the way David, what chair was he seated in?"

"Murther, Bishop, Murther."

CHAPTER 20

The station looked like it was out of a PBS Sherlock Holmes program. We had pulled into one of many slots for the trains, all under a giant roof. It was a gigantic pergola. The slots for each train were made by the platforms that extended along the track for many cars. The engines were all facing the end of the building. To our left, still inside the building were many double decker buses. Most of the people leaving the train boarded these. It was very crowded in the station. We weren't the only train that had arrived. At the front of the building there was a restaurant, a bookstore, and another shop. On the right there was offices, bathrooms, and the way out.

Patrick led the way off the train. He wove his way through the crowd quickly. He had soon outdistanced Cliona and I. "We'd better hurry and catch him, Cliona."

"No need, Colleen. He's only going to get a taxi for us. We'll meet him outside."

"Oh good. I wondered why he took off in such a rush."

"That's just his way. He has always hurried, even as a child."

"Is the station always this crowded?"

"It is very busy whenever I'm here. The trains a very convenient to us in the South. I imagine it is as convenient to people in the West, as well."

"Well it is marvelous. A very romantic way to travel. Our trains are very modern and barren. The train stations are a wreck. They used to be very beautiful, but they haven't been kept up."

We had reached the entrance to the station and stepped out into the day. Patrick was to our right, and had a cab waiting for us. All three of us quietly got in. Patrick told the driver that we were going to 58 Montgomery Mews. The cab swung out into the traffic, which was even worse than Cork. We drove West along the river for a few blocks. Both sides of the river were lined with very old buildings. Most needed a good cleaning and paint. They were ornate and few were over four or five stories tall. We passed a number of graceful bridges. They had low arches, which offered a sense of elegance to the view down the river.

"Colleen, do you see that building across the river ahead of us? The one with the dome."

"Yes I do Patrick."

"That is the Four Courts. It is similar to your Supreme Court Building in Washington DC. It was designed by James Gandon who designed many of the best buildings in Dublin.

"It looks very classical, particularly the dome."

"As are most of Dublin's fine buildings, and homes, for that matter, the Four Courts is Georgian. Mother, isn't Georgian Neo-Classical?"

"Yes it is Patrick"

"Well there you are Colleen. You were right. It is

Classical."

The cab had turned right and gone up a hill. This part of the city was very similar to Cork. Lots of old buildings and shops. Just like Cork, the sidewalks were busy with people. We turned left and joined a messy flow of traffic. I was very glad that I wasn't driving in this. We made a few more turns. I was totally confused by now. I couldn't tell, for the life of me, what direction we were going.

The cab had been driving down a road not much larger than an alley when we turned left onto a very wide street. It seemed to be about six lanes wide, and border a fenced park. The road followed the park around the block, turning 90 degrees to the right. At the entrance was a small sign that read "St. Stephen's Green." For a moment I could glance inside the park. It was very green. I thought I glimpsed water in the center. Certainly there were many trees, and even more people. The park looked friendly, an inviting place.

Across from the park we passed the Shelbourne Hotel. There were many fancy cars double and tripled parked in front. We had to weave around them. The steps of the hotel were busy with very well dressed people coming and going, a lot of money here. The road turned into an alley at the end of the hotel. We drove in only to emerge after a couple of blocks. We were back on a wide road with two-way traffic. There were many shops and small businesses in the restored Georgian Homes that lined the street. We had gone only a few more blocks when we crossed one of the elegant bridges. I was confused. I thought that we had been going away from the river all the while. "Cliona? How did we get back to the river? I thought we were headed away from it."

"We did Colleen. That is the Grand Canal we just crossed. We're South of the Liffey by quite a bit now." The cab passed through another small shopping district, and then turned left into a warren of narrow streets. We turned into an even narrower street and pulled in front of a stone wall with a gate. Actually it had a small gate and a large double gate. We all got out. Cliona and I stood around while Patrick and the cabby unloaded our bags. Patrick paid the man, went over to the small gate and unlocked it. I grabbed my bag and followed Patrick and Cliona through the gate.

Another world, I had stepped into another world. It is the only way I can describe what I saw. I was standing in a courtyard facing the main section of an L shaped stone cottage. To my left was the L. It was all glass on the front with French doors facing the courtyard.

I could see a giant sideboard and a matching giant wooden dining table with at least a dozen chairs inside the glass L. In the middle of the courtyard was a large fig tree offset towards the dining area. I suppose it was offset to leave room for a car to be parked behind the large double doors. The branches of the tree spread out to cover the whole courtyard. It reminded me of the giant Banyan Tree covering the courtyard at the Moana Surfrider in Honolulu. It wasn't anywhere near that big though.

The main part of the cottage had small mullioned windows with intricate leaded glass. The front door was a traditional Irish double door painted a brilliant red. In front of the French doors were three very wide steps that extended the whole length of the L. Except for the area in front of the French doors the steps were covered with potted plants of every size. The contrast between the gray stone of the building and walls with the brilliant colors of the flowers gave the place a feeling of magic. It made me feel happy.

"Cliona this is a marvelous place. Oh! You've painted this haven't you? I've seen it in your house. I can't remember where, but I know I've seen it in your house."

"I have indeed. Many times, if the truth were to be known. This is a very special place for me, both as an artist and personally. I never cease to be amazed at Aunt Maude. She has no artistic talent and little sense of design. Yet... she has achieved a balance, a harmony here that is incomparable. I paint this courtyard as often as I can, in as many combinations of season, time of day, light and weather conditions as I possibly can. I've yet to repeat myself."

All of us went into the house. The main hall was very narrow with many doors leading off from it. Patrick took the first door to the right so I followed him. It was a bedroom. "This is for you Colleen. You can leave your bags here. The woman will come in to unpack."

"The Woman! What woman, Patrick. Doesn't she have a name?"

"Well of course she does. Don't be so testy. I don't happen to know her name. She is a friend of Aunt Maude's who fell on hard times, so Maude has her do little things around the house as an excuse for giving her money, which Maude is rolling in. Now follow me." A little sheepishly, I followed Patrick back into the hall and into the glorious dining room that I had seen from the courtyard. As we entered the room I could see that there was a couch and a couple of armchairs at the far end that I couldn't see from the courtyard. "This is where everyone gathers Colleen. There is a drawing room, but it is very tiny, and dark, and windowless. I haven't been in it since I was a small boy. Most likely neither has anyone else. I'll just go help mother, then I'm off to the library. I'll meet you and mother for dinner. Have a grand time shopping."

"Thanks Patrick I will."

With that he left the room. I could hear the two of them in the back of the house. Soon I heard Patrick leave. When he had gone Cliona shouted out to me.

"Will I fix us some tea? It'll be ready in just a tic. We can walk into town when we've finished."

"That would be very nice." Cliona soon came into the room with the tea on a tray. We both drank rather quickly. I was anxious to see more of Dublin, and I think Cliona was anxious to show me. Both of us put our cups down together. Cliona laughed.

"Are you as ready to go as I am? I am hoping you will like Dublin. It is a very elegant city in many ways. Tarnished a bit with life, but more interesting as a result."

"Yes, Cliona. I don't know why I am looking forward to this so very much, but I am." Cliona grabbed an umbrella and we left.

CHAPTER 21

Cliona set a good pace. I had trouble keeping up with her. We walked, briskly, back the way we had driven. Soon we were walking through a shopping district. It didn't seem to be more than a block or two long, but was very busy never the less. There was a Seven Eleven across the street. It wasn't a US Seven Eleven, but looked like it was the same kind of store. Ahead, at the end of the shopping area, was the Canal that I had thought was the river. We walked across the arched bridge, and stopped in the middle of the Canal. "This is the Grand Canal, Colleen. Look to the West and you can see the locks. It wasn't used for many years after the railroads came, and became quite an eyesore. Some years ago people started working on restoring small sections."

"They have done a wonderful job here. Do many boats use it?"

"I don't know. You can catch one of the restored Canal Barges somewhere here in Dublin and ride out to Palmertsown for an evening. It is very dear so I have never done it. You do see boats moored along the canal, but I don't think I've ever seen one moving, but look, look."

"Where, Cliona?"

"Back up the canal. See the horses coming along the old tow road? I have not seen anyone riding along here since I was a very young girl. That is quite magnificent.

"It is an amazing sight. Where do you think they keep the horses?"

"They must be from quite a ways back up the canal. The only places in town are the old mews that were used to stable horses for the Georgian homes before the automobile. Those are all converted into expensive homes and cottages now. Well we should continue. We'll walk back to St. Stephan's Green. The better shops are all just North of the park."

We hurried along. As soon as we had crossed the canal the street changed to a business area. There were a few shops, but they were to serve the businesses that were in the old Georgian Homes that had been converted to offices. At the head of the street it narrowed into the canyon again and we were soon approaching St. Stephan's Green.

"Come along Colleen. We'll walk to the other corner of the park and then turn into Grafton Street. Brown Thomas will be our first stop." We pressed on. I was surprised to find that Grafton Street was closed to traffic. The street was fairly narrow and filled with people. We hadn't gone more than a few hundred feet when I almost stepped on a man who was drawing a large religious looking face on the sidewalk with colored chalk. He had a small box along with his supplies beside him. A few people had dropped coins into the hat. A great many more were milling around, taking a look at the work he was doing.

A couple of blocks further and we were in front of Brown Thomas. The outside appeared to be many similar stores. There was the typical window framed in mahogany, but instead of just one window and one door, there were many windows, and many doors. The displays in the windows were very attractive, but subdued. We went in the first pair of doors that we came to. We had to go down a few stairs since the floor in the store was a little lower than street level. We were surrounded by cosmetics. Cliona quickly led us through the cosmetic section. On our left was another department, ladies dresses, from the looks of it. We had to step up a stair to get in to see the dresses. Cliona charged on not stopping for a moment. At the far end of this department was a staircase. Cliona made a beeline for it. I hurriedly followed as she almost ran up the stairs. Once on the floor above I could see almost the whole length of the store. Each department was on a slightly different level than another. Thinking about the store front and how it looked, many store front windows joined together, and the different floor levels inside, I got the distinct impression that Brown Thomas was just that, many different stores joined together.

Cliona stopped outside what appeared to be a small restaurant. "This is the Brown Thomas tea room, Colleen. No trip to Dublin would be complete without seeing it." The room was filled with blue haired ladies buzzing with the day's stories. The clink of the cups and their saucers with the hiss of the steam in the urns brought back memories of Manning's Cafeterias in Portland when I was a little girl. "I wanted you to see this piece of

Dublin, Colleen. There are probably few places on earth still like this."

As the customers entered they picked up a tray which was then slid along chromium rails past the goodies being offered. The first station was glasses of juices set in shaved ice. No cans of reconstituted concentrate here. Just next to the juices were the sandwiches, each carefully arranged on a china plate. Behind this counter were young girls with white jackets, like a butcher might wear, and a white maid's hat. They bustled about filling empty spaces as the various juices, sandwiches, and other delights were taken off by the hungry customers.

Now we can go see the galleries on Dawson Street." Cliona turned and started to leave, but stopped and turned back to face me. I'm sorry Colleen. Would you like to stay and shop a bit?"

"It looks very interesting, Cliona, but I'd rather go see the galleries with you. And if we could, could we go to a bookstore?"

"A bookstore? We can of course. It's fairly late in the day, you know. We'll go to Fogarty's on Green Street. The atmosphere is marvelous, absolutely Dickensian. I always expect to meet Jonathan Swift browsing through one of the back rooms."

"Yes, yes, that's exactly what I'd like to see. Portland has a great used bookstore, Aldyke's, but it doesn't seem like an old bookstore. The shelves are very utilitarian. In fact, the whole place is very utilitarian, lots of plywood."

We had left the store and were walking up the street. I could barely move there were so many people. My shoulders rubbed against people going the other way.

A man turned in front of me to go into a store, almost knocking me down. "Sorry maam." People moved at their own pace. A mother with twins in a stroller moved slowly and carefully ahead of me. I followed letting her break the crowd like the bow of a giant ship. Finally I left the sidewalk and was walking up the center of the street, just to be walking in the middle of a street I think. It seemed like it was more crowded here than on the sidewalk. I wasn't the only one to defy convention. A mild act of defiance, but defiance nevertheless. I glanced over at Cliona. She had a small grin on her face as she watched me. She understood. As I returned her smile I saw him, or thought I saw him. He was back in the crowd, the Superintendent. He was watching me intently, but when he saw me looking back he turned and quickly withdrew into the crowd. I turned to follow him, gesturing to Cliona to come with me. She looked puzzled, but joined me. It was hopeless. He was nowhere to be seen, so I stopped. Cliona came up alongside me.

"What is the matter Colleen?"

"I spotted Superintendent Mundell following us. The minute he saw that I had seen him he turned and disappeared into the crowd. If he is so suspicious of me why wouldn't he have me followed by somebody I don't know. It doesn't make a lot of sense."

"Are you sure it was the Superintendent? Did you get a really good look at him?

"Only for a second, but I'm almost sure it was him. It doesn't make any sense though unless, of course Patrick was right, and the Superintendent is somehow mixed up in all of this. I've called Portland like Patrick suggested. The policeman I wanted to talk to wasn't there, but his secretary remembered that Dad had called about someone, and she said it could have been Mundell." We had been walking as we talked and soon reached the bookstore. I was a little disappointed. The front of the store was no more than twenty feet across. It was painted a lime green, or I should say had been painted a lime green. The paint had peeled off in many places.

Once inside my impression didn't change. We were in a small room with all the current magazines, candy bars, newspapers, and cigarettes for sale. To say I was disappointed would be an understatement. I was standing looking around when I saw Cliona next to a small door with a knowing smile on her face. "Come through here Colleen. You'll find it worthwhile."

I followed her into the next room, and saw what I would call a movie version of a bookstore. The room was not large, but there were at least two doorways leading to other rooms. There was a balcony on three sides of the room with two spiral staircases leading to the balcony. Each wall of the room, and the balcony, was lined with bookcases, floor to ceiling. In the center of the room were display cases with open books. Walking into the next room I saw that it was almost the same as the first. The wall ahead of me however was all windows, facing a courtyard filled with tables. People were reading at the tables. There was obviously a restaurant in the courtyard since everyone had a drink and something to eat. Next to the window were two doors that led to other rooms, one on the left and another on the right.

"This is perfect, Cliona. I couldn't have imagined a better bookstore."

"I thought you'd be pleased. Why don't you look

around as much as you'd like? We have a couple of hours until we need to meet Patrick for dinner. I have someone I want to see, but I'll be back in no more than an hour or so."

"OK I'll see you when you get back. Look for me in the courtyard. I'll probably look around for awhile. Then I'll buy something and take it in there and read it. I couldn't possibly leave here without taking advantage.

CHAPTER 22

I had wandered from room to room for a while. Each room had books on a different subject matter. Actually a better way to say it was that all of the books on one subject could be found in a single room, since some rooms had many subjects. Finally I saw an old book on Irish History. I bought the book and went into the courtyard. There was a small bar at one end that had drinks, sandwiches, and pastries. I bought a coffee and a sweet roll, chose a table and settled down to read.

I must have really been engrossed. Cliona was standing over me saying, "Are you ready to go Colleen? I'm sorry I was so late. We just have a few minutes before we're supposed to meet Patrick."

"I'm ready. What time is it? I was so involved in this book that it seems like you left just a few minutes ago."

"It's half seven, or close anyway. We were supposed to meet Patrick at half-seven at "Joseph's on the Green." Fortunately it's not far."

I got up, and we left. When we got to the street it was dark and had started to drizzle. We moved along quickly dodging the umbrellas. It was a good thing I had grown up in the Pacific Northwest. My umbrella dodging instincts worked well. It only took a few minutes to retrace our route. Soon we were inside a very cozy restaurant. There was a reception area that looked like a lobby of a small hotel. A fire was going in an ornate fireplace that was the focal point of several large armchairs. We shook ourselves, and an attendant helped us off with our coats.

"Will we sit in front of the fire Colleen? Patrick should be along any minute."

"That would be very nice."

We sat facing the door so we could see Patrick when he arrived. The attendant gave us each a menu. I glanced at it quickly. There were many different kinds of fish. I hadn't heard of many of them, Brill, Bream, and John Dory. Salmon I knew. There was one chicken entree, and one lamb, but no beef. I glanced up and saw a morose Patrick enter: Right on his heels was Liam grinning from car to ear.

"Look who I found Cliona. Your son is not his usual charming self, but I told him I would join you and make up for it."

Patrick mumbled something and plopped himself into a chair across from me. He immediately immersed himself in the menu. Liam had to bring over another chair which he placed facing me sort of in front of Patrick. I wasn't all that pleased to see Liam. I wanted to talk to Patrick about seeing the Superintendent, and to go over Patrick's theory of the Superintendent as the murderer. The way Liam had acted the night before kept me from saying anything. Liam and Cliona were happily chatting away. Patrick was slumped low into his chair. His nose had not come out of the menu since he got here. I was trying to think of a way to get Patrick off to myself. Finally a waiter came in to take our order, which meant that we had to read the menu in earnest. The waiter took both Cliona and my order and then turned to Liam. "Now I'll not stay to eat. I only wanted to talk to Colleen for a minute, but I think this isn't the best time. Enjoy your meal. Colleen can I call on you tomorrow?

"You c-cannot," bellowed Patrick as rose in his chair. "You s-s-shloother. You've no need to bother her again."

"He most certainly can," I retorted. "And what business is it of yours anyway."

Liam chuckled and turned to leave. "I'll give you a call tomorrow Colleen."

He left with both Cliona and I staring at Patrick in disbelief. "Whatever has gotten into you Patrick," asked his mother.

"I don't know mother. Liam was... he just forced himself along. I found the trip rewarding. I discovered a couple of small items that I hadn't known at the library, and I was looking forward to telling you about them. I also wanted to talk about the Superintendent again. I know my misgivings about the Superintendent are probably without foundation. Still, I wanted to talk about it some more. With Liam along I couldn't. And he just would not take a hint and his behavior last night was reprehensible."

"How do you know what his behavior was last night, Patrick? I don't recall you being along, or my telling you anything at all."

"I don't know I suppose. It's just that I walked over to ask you to dinner and saw the two of you driving off. I know it's none of my business. I've no right, no right at all to act the way I am. Sorry, I'll behave.

"Well that's all right then. Anyway, I want to talk about your theory, Patrick," I said excitedly. "I saw him following us today."

"You what?"

"I saw the Superintendent following us up the street with all the shops."

"Up Grafton street, Patrick. But Colleen only caught a glimpse. It may as well have been someone else.

"It may have been, but I." All of a sudden I remembered the waiter who was patiently standing behind us waiting for Patrick's order. "Patrick you'd better order so this man can get on with his work."

"What man? Oh, oh the waiter. Of course." He gave the waiter his order and turned back to me. "I also wanted to tell you about Aunt Maude. She's a gas woman. Has mother told you anything about her?"

"No Patrick, but what about the Superintendent?"

"Can we wait until after dinner? I want to have my thoughts sorted."

"Sure Patrick. Tell me about your Aunt Maude then. Who's Aunt is she? Yours Patrick or Cliona's?"

"She's my sister Colleen. A brilliant women, but more than a little unconventional."

"OK. What did you want to tell me."

"I think only that she has gone off to Africa."

"That doesn't sound very unconventional to me. Nuns go to Africa."

"I know, I know, but you see she's gone after her

lover. He's 65 and fell in love with a twenty-year-old nurse. The two of them ran off to Africa, and now Maude has gone after them."

"How old is Maude?"

"She's sixty four."

"I see. Well then I assume since you said "lover" that they are not married. Has he then supported her all these years, or does she work?"

"Maude has been in the theater all these years, and has done quite well, I might add. She has had many patrons over the course of the years. The house where we are staying was a gift from one. But she never was overly concerned when they would go back to their wives. There were always many waiting to fill the last fella's spot. Until now that is. You see..." Just then the waiter appeared and asked us to come in. We followed him through a few rooms, each with no more than four tables or so. It was like the bookstore and like Brown Thomas. The restaurant was made by combining many small stores. He sat us at a round table, and left.

"Anyway as I was saying, Maude had many supporters, and to say she didn't work is unfair. She was in many productions. Some were quite outstanding. All of my life I have admired her greatly."

As we were talking the waiter brought us our first course. We must have been very hungry since not another word was spoken until we had all finished. As soon as we were done our places were cleared and the next course was brought in. Both Cliona and Patrick had ordered the soup. I had a sorbet, which I quickly finished. "Maude sounds delightful to me. It's too bad I didn't get to meet her." They both made noises of agreement as they tackled their soup. I shut up. The last course was served and we all dug in.

Once again not a word was spoken. As I finished I had an almost uncontrollable urge to lean back with a contented smile and belch. I didn't, but it was close. Soon both Patrick and Cliona finished. "Well," said Patrick as he too leaned back, the front legs of his chair leaving the ground. He had a look on his face that said belch to me, but he apparently thought better of it because he returned his chair to the floor. "Well now, you think you saw the Inspector. That is very interesting. I still think that note in the margin "Check up on the Super" or whatever it said might have some connection. Just how well did you see him Colleen?"

"Thinking back on it, not all that well. I only looked at him for a few seconds. But if it wasn't him why did the person turn away so quickly the minute they noticed I was watching?"

"That could have been coincidental Colleen," piped in Cliona. "You know, he was turning away for a very good reason, and hadn't seen you at all."

"Or was only admiring your good looks, and turned away when he saw that you had caught him out." Saying this, Patrick blushed the color of a tomato. Cliona and I spoke at the same time. I tried to say thank you, but Cliona was the more forceful. "So that's why you were so cross with Liam." I finally got out "Patrick that is very sweet of you, but I am not at all attracted to Liam, except perhaps as a friend. I much prefer taller academic types." Now it was my turn to blush.

"Look at the two of you. You might as well be children. What am I to do with you? Patrick looked at us both, and grinned. "Why don't we discuss my theory that the Superintendent might be the culprit? It all hinges around that note in the margin. Have you checked your house at all Cliona?"

"No I didn't. I thought we had left it that your theory wasn't plausible, so I didn't check at all, but I did call Portland. The man that I wanted to talk to wasn't in, but his secretary remembered that Dad had called about something. She also thought that it may have had something to do with somebody named Mundell, but she wasn't sure."

"I still don't think it too likely, but since you may have seen him today wouldn't it be worth your time to have a quick look about the house. You should check back in Portland again," Patrick added.

"What more would I check for, Patrick?"

"Anything that might indicate he was suspicious about the Superintendent; notes, uh, phone calls to the US, the missing pages maybe."

"I'll look around the house, but I can't imagine that the police missed much. I've called a buddy of Dad's on the force in Portland. If he did do any checking it would have been through this guy. This really doesn't seem any more plausible now than it did before, except Dad may have been asking Novak to look something up for him. If only I hadn't seen him. It was him too, not somebody else. I'm sure of that."

"If you two have that sorted could we go back to Maude's? It's getting quite late, and we should catch the early train back to Mallow in the morning."

CHAPTER 23

He'd been following her since he'd first seen them in Grafton Street. It was bad luck, all right, that she had turned and looked at him. Whether or not she had recognized him, he left as quickly as he could. If it wasn't too conspicuous he would have run, but he remained calm, and quietly walked back the way that he had come. Would it be too dangerous to go back and try to find them again? Would they be looking for him? In the end he decided they would. His pace quickened as he decided to stop in at Dublin Castle, and meet with his boss. There could be no question then as to why he was in Dublin, if it ever came to that. As Chief Superintendent he couldn't take any chances.

He walked quickly and was at the Castle in no time. He signed in and found that his boss wasn't there. It mattered little. His presence was explained and recorded. When he left he had a strange urge to find them again, but he resisted and slowly walked back to his hotel. It actually was a small guesthouse in Ballsbridge, just across the street from the Berkeley Court. It was close to where they were staying and close to the DART station. He had followed them when they left walking a discreet distance behind them. Now he didn't need to be careful so he walked to the Tara Street DART Station and took the train to the Landsdowne Road Station. The Superintendent got off the train and walked up the street to his hotel.

Once in his room he took off his coat, loosened his tie, and sat. Now that he was here, and had been discovered, he was doubting why he had come at all. In fact looking back on it there didn't seem to be one good reason to be in Dublin. What had he hoped to accomplish? His attempts so far had been miserable failures. This was the worst. He'd better go back and develop a real plan, he decided. None of this running of half cocked with no idea in mind of what he'd actually do if he succeeded. He couldn't imagine what he would do if she confronted him. It would be all over then. This trip was madness. He was quite the fool to have tried it. It could have accomplished very little at best, and now it may all be at jeopardy.

He packed his things, checked out, and took the train back to Mallow.

CHAPTER 24

Our return to Maude's and the train ride back to Mallow the next morning had been uneventful. Mary Igoe was not overly late picking us up. She dropped us all in front of Cliona's house. I thanked them both and went inside Dad's house. I was strangely tired and didn't feel much like company. I wasn't looking forward to searching the house again, so I put it off for a bit and fixed a cup of coffee. Seeing the Superintendent was so weird. I couldn't say that it upset me, but it certainly had given me pause to think. And Liam had certainly upset Patrick. Over me? I think he was only getting Patrick's goat, and anyway I was becoming quite fond of Patrick.

I certainly was not looking for a relationship with anyone in Ireland. I didn't plan on being here much longer. My job wouldn't wait forever. But if I was, I could see Patrick and I. Yes easily, and judging by his reaction last night he was interested. Anyway, I had to stop this musing and start searching. I didn't know for what, but I would look anyway. I went through each room carefully leaving Dad's study until last. I thought that if I found anything it would be there, but I wanted to cross off the rest of the house first. And cross it off I did.

I found nothing.

The door to the study stood slightly ajar. Hesitantly I entered, not knowing where to start. The desk was the most likely place to find something, I thought. So, I started with the bookshelves. I didn't for a minute think that Dad had installed a secret hiding place, but I tapped the walls, and felt for levers dutifully. After a good hour of searching I had found nothing, big surprise. Only the desk was left. As I was about to start Patrick peeked his head in the door. "How's it going, Colleen?"

"Oh, hi Patrick. I've found nothing so far. There's only the desk left. I really don't expect to find anything. I'll keep looking though."

"Have you checked in Portland to see if your father sent anything home?"

"Not yet. They're all asleep. I'll call early this evening."

"Right. Don't forget the Hooley tonight, and come over for tea. That's really why I came over - to invite you. Mother has made soda biscuits, and they're even better than usual."

"Thanks, I'll be over in a minute, just as soon as I've searched Dad's desk." Patrick left and I started going through the drawers. There was nothing out of the ordinary that I could see. All of the drawers seemed the right length, no secret compartments. The last drawer I searched was the lap drawer. Like the others it contained nothing unusual, but when I went to push it back in it was very hard to get in. I pulled it back out, and removed it. As I pulled it free of the desk an envelope fell to the ground. I gasped. This was not something that I had expected. Carefully I put the drawer down and picked up the envelope. It was full of papers, and a letter, a letter from me to Dad. I quickly went through the rest. Dad had saved all the letters that I had written, all three of them. It wasn't the answer to a mystery, but I was very moved.

I could feel the tears come to my eyes. Why hadn't I written more? Three letters in a year didn't say much for me. I sat down and reread each letter. None of them said very much. Couldn't I have spent more time? It was too late now. I started to bawl again. I just couldn't help it. After a few minutes I calmed down. Taking my letters with me, I went into my room and put them with my papers. In the bathroom I cleaned up, and then I went over to Cliona's for tea.

Cliona answered her door. "Colleen, are you all right? Come in, come in." She didn't give me a chance to explain. She just led me by the arm into the Drawing Room. Patrick looked up with a concerned look on his face. He rose and came over to me bringing a cup of tea with him. "Now," he said as he handed me the tea. Patrick sat down beside me half turned towards me. Cliona had sat in the chair across from us. They both had the most concerned look on their faces. "You two are something else. You'd think I'd just endured another tragedy. Actually, in its own way it was a tragedy. Look, when I was searching the house I found the only three letters I'd written Dad since he came over here. It just made me very sad that I had written so little. Thanks for your concern, but I'll be OK."

"Well," Patrick exhaled. "Well indeed," said Cliona. "Will you tell Colleen what you found at the library?" At the mention of his research Patrick brightened considerably. "I will, of course. Now, It was only a wee thing I found, but very interesting. There are a few notes on Assolas house that one of the Bourkes submitted sometime last century. According to the notes I saw yesterday it would seem that General Taafe was at Assolas having his tea while the battle at Knocknanuss was being fought. This is a direct contradiction to all the history books. Although, God knows, there is little enough about Knocknanuss in any of them."

"Is this important Patrick?"

"I'm not at all sure, Colleen. The man that holds the Hoolies has hinted that it might be quite worth my while to attend tonight. He probably has found someone with local knowledge about the battle. I'm hoping to corroborate the story about General Taafe and possibly even discover what significance it may have had. I can find precious little about General Taafe. His absence at the battle, if indeed he was absent, may have been to our advantage"

"I'm looking forward to tonight, Patrick. I'm still invited aren't I?"

"You are of course. It should be a grand evening, great craic."

"What?"

"I know, I know, that term makes Americans nervous. Craic in Irish is good conversation, not drugs."

"I knew that. I just forgot, sorry. I think I'll wander back over to Dad's. I still haven't called home to see if Dad started anything concerning the Superintendent. I'll let you know if I find anything out. There was nothing in the house, just like I said. Bye."

I walked back to Dad's. I really wanted to be

alone for awhile. I appreciated their concern, but I wanted to remember Dad by myself. I would be sad. Oh, I would be very sad, but it would be my final good-bye, this day in Ireland, this gray day, this very gray day in Ireland. I went into the house, into the bedroom and collapsed on the bed. My soul cried out for my Father, but "qouth the raven, nevermore." I cried the tears of Emer, and slept.

CHAPTER 25

I was playing a loud drum. The pounding got louder and quicker. I woke with a start. Someone was pounding at the front door. I got out of bed and groggily glanced at the clock. It was 3:00 in the afternoon. I really hadn't slept for very long, but I couldn't remember when I had lain down. I pulled my robe about me and went to the front door. I could hear Patrick calling to me through the closed door. I opened the door to see Patrick with a very concerned look on his face.

"There you are. Are you all right, Colleen? I must have been knocking for ten minutes."

"'I'm fine Patrick. I must have really fallen asleep. I was dreaming about playing a giant drum. It must have been your knocking. Well don't just stand there, come in." Patrick followed me back into the drawing room. I sat down on the couch. Patrick stood looking uncertain. "Sit Patrick, please. I'm still trying to get the cobwebs out. Boy I must have been totally gone. You can take that look off your face. There is nothing to be concerned about. Oh, we're still going to the Hooley tonight, aren't we?"

"We are, of course, but I had an idea for the afternoon. Have I mentioned that the bones of all of the dead at Knocknanuss are buried in the catacombs of the old church in Buttevant? I'm asking because I was reminded of it when I was in the library in Dublin."

"I don't remember you saying anything about it Patrick, but right now I'm not sure if I remember my name."

"Your name's Colleen, or at least that is what you claim."

"Thank you Patrick, very kind of you. Now, what about these bones, and what do they have to do with this afternoon?"

"I thought we might take a drive North to Buttevant. There is a lovely old Abbey on the way, Ballybeag, and the old church in Buttevant is in a lovely setting along the Awbeg. We could stop for dinner at a wonderful old pub in Buttevant for dinner. It would make a great start for the evening."

"But old bones? In a catacomb. And how would I get dressed for tonight. I don't know Patrick. Old Bones?"

"It was just an idea. I suppose not a very good one, sorry."

I'd hurt his feelings. It was written all over his face. He was so easily hurt. Liam certainly wouldn't have been phased, but I prefer Patrick's sensitivity even though it means I'll have to be more careful. "Oh no, Patrick, I think I would enjoy going to the old church. I just have to think what I can wear that will work for tonight as well as this afternoon." Only partially a white lie.

"You would? I mean you want to go? That's

marvelous. Look, we could easily return here in time for you to change for tonight."

The look on Patrick's face was one of pure joy. He certainly had counted on my acceptance. Why was this so important to him? I certainly could put up with a few old bones if it made him this happy. "When do you want to go, Patrick?"

"As soon as you're ready. I've got everything we'll need in the car."

"Let me run a brush through my hair. I hope you don't mind if I stay in these clothes. I slept in them, but they're perfect for catacombs. Oh, what about the pub? Do I look all right for dinner."

"You're fine, you're fine, the lads will have quite a treat."

"Patrick!"

"They will. It's a local sort of a place, mostly frequented by regulars. You'll be a standout."

"That's a compliment."

"It is indeed, Colleen. Now, will we go?"

"We will go, and thank you." Patrick smiled, but didn't reply. Before long we had driven back into Mallow, and were proceeding north from the roundabout. The trip into Mallow was becoming so familiar. It didn't seem to take any time at all. We passed a Toyota dealership as we left Mallow. It was surprisingly like a Toyota dealership back home. I'm not sure why it was surprising. Maybe Toyota dealerships look the same worldwide. In fact they probably did. The road narrowed, and dropped into a valley. It had been very wide with long straight stretches, and sweeping curves as we left town, but now it twisted every which way. We hadn't been in the valley very long when it flattened out on the right. As we came around a bend I could see stone ruins of a church in the middle of a field.

"Is this where the catacombs are, Patrick?"

"No Colleen. They are ahead in the middle of the town. What you're looking at is the ruins of Ballybeag Abbey. Cromwell had the Abbey razed as his army marched through this part of Ireland. It had been a Cistercian Abbey, and was a great center of learning. In fact the folk history claims it was originally one of the Celtic Universities. It probably had been teaching the Fili since before the birth of Christ. Many of the original monasteries were just that."

"The Fili? Who are the Fili?"

"They were the learned men of Ireland, the lawyers, the poets, and the historians. The lawyers were called Brehon, the poets Fili, and the historians were called Seanachi. There were levels of achievement as well, probably similar to our current degrees. The highest level of achievement was called, uh, actually the people the achieved the highest level were called Olamh. In the old culture there was no writing, that came with Christianity. So, everything was taught verbally. It took nine years to achieve the level of Olamh."

"That is amazing, Patrick. I hadn't known that there were universities in Ireland before Queens University and Trinity. In fact I've always thought that the Sorbonne was the oldest university in existence. You know that is ridiculous when you think of it. The Chinese, the ancient Egyptians, all old societies would have had places of learning for their ruling classes."

While I was talking Patrick had driven into the

center of a small village. It appeared to be a one street town. The road was quite a bit wider than Mallow giving the town, actually a village, a spacious look. The buildings looked very much the same as in Mallow. We pulled over in front of a nice stone church. It was fairly large, but not the size of a Cathedral. "This doesn't look old enough to have catacombs, Patrick."

"It doesn't, Colleen. Look beyond the square." Patrick pointed slightly behind us. The church was along the street. You entered from a square with a fountain in the center. Beyond the square was a lawn leading to a riverbank. Just behind where we were parked, and across the lawn was an ancient church. It had no roof. There were plants growing on the inside their tendrils poking out the window openings, long abandoned by glass. "Now that looks like a church with catacombs, Patrick. It could be a movie set, if only the sky was black with lightning flashing, and great rolls of thunder."

"I've never notice that, Colleen, but it certainly does indeed. I think we are so used to our ruins in Ireland that we don't truly appreciate their drama. Do you mind waiting here while I go for keys? I should have called and made arrangements, but I didn't so I need to organize that."

"I think I will wander around the grounds if you don't mind Patrick. It looks very pretty down by the river."

"Of course, of course, I'll find you easily enough."

Patrick got out of the car and went off in the direction of the Church. I got out and wandered down to the river. The grass on the lawn was not cut very short. It looked more like a meadow than a lawn. The bank of the river was not at all steep, allowing a good view of the water when I was no more than halfway across. The water was swifter than I had expected. Not quite a mountain stream, still the ripples in the water flashed as the sun caught each. Across the river the bank was wooded. There were a few willows just back from the bank, which was steeper on that side, but mostly that bank was lined with clumps of hawthorn, spindly rhododendrons, and birch. Here where I was the lawn went down to the edge of the water. As it got closer to the old church the bank became steeper like the other side, and wooded. I sat in the grass waiting for Patrick, watching the water dance in the sun. I was half-asleep from the warmth when I heard Patrick come up behind me.

"You are a perfect picture sitting there, Colleen. I've often wished I had mother's talent for painting. This would be an impressive painting. Shall we go in? I have the keys." Patrick bent over offering me his hand. It was an elegant and gentle gesture. I was touched. Somehow I now knew that everything would turn out all right. Patrick pulled me to my feet, and we walked over to the door to the old church. Patrick unlocked the padlock, a very modern looking lock that was totally out of place clasping the ancient black chain that held the doors shut. We swung open one of the doors and went in. We were in a small stone courtyard facing two more doors that were also chained together. Next to us, in the wall on our left was a small wooden door that was slightly ajar.

"Patrick, why is this all locked up? We could have easily crawled in through any of the windows."

"We could have indeed, but if we had we still

would be unable to enter the catacombs. This small door here is where we enter. They really don't care if people wander about most of the church, but fear, rightly so, that soon all of the bodies would be carted off bit by bit if they didn't protect them."

"That's ghoulish, but probably right. Let's go in now. I don't know if I can if I think about it much more. I'm feeling a little squeamish."

"You could stay here while I go in, Colleen. I won't be but a moment. I really only want to look around to see if it warrants a return."

"No, I'm OK. I've come this far. I'll kick myself later if I don't go." Patrick smiled, nodded his head, took my hand and in we went. The stairs spiraled down to the left. It appeared that no one had been down the stairs for quite awhile. When we reached the bottom the stairs emptied into a long chamber. We stepped forward, hesitantly, amazed at the amount of light. The room seemed to go the length of the church. Along each side were many shallow chambers formed by Romanesque arches that went most of the way up the wall. On top of these arches where many short arches that held up the building above us. Each of these arches had no sides forming a window to the outside at their very top. The room smelled a little musty, but I didn't feel apprehensive any more. I think the light made it a lot less scary.

"Will we look in a few of the chambers, Colleen?

"Sure, I'm game. I don't feel squeamish anymore."

"Good."

He squeezed my hand and we walked over to the first chamber. It was filled with bones, very old bones, all wrapped in dusty, tattered, black cloth. Actually the cloth was gray now, but looked as though it had been black. The bodies were carefully stacked. A few had no heads, the skulls having detached and rolled onto the floor. It wasn't scary at all. We walked along looking in three or four more of the chambers. They were all the same. "I've seen quite enough, Colleen. We can leave when you're through.

"We can leave now then. I'm glad I came down here, but there isn't any atmosphere. It seems… I don't know, kind of clean maybe. I expected very dark caverns, with drips of moisture on the walls, a few barely burning torches on the wall."

"And maybe the clank of chains. No, no not the clank of chains, a skeleton draped over his chains where he had been anchored to the wall centuries ago."

"That's it, Patrick, and the moan of a prisoner deeper in the dungeon. Instead we find neatly stacked bones bathed in light, a little disappointing. I think I wanted to feel squeamish."

"I know what you mean. Now, we're out." We had an awkward moment as we came out still holding hands. I didn't want to be the one to let go and neither did Patrick, but one of us had to be the first. We had things to do. Finally I lessened my grip. Patrick took the cue and we let go. I felt like I was still in High School. I couldn't think of a thing to say. At last Patrick spoke. Will we go to O'Meara's? I think it might be a little early for dinner. But if we eat now, I can easily return you to your Dad's in time to change for tonight."

"Let's go. I could eat a horse. I can't imagine why seeing all of those skeletons made me hungry, but it did." I started to get into the car, but Patrick stopped me, and pointed across the street. Hanging over the door of one of the drabbest looking shops I had ever seen was a new sign. It was one of those hand painted signs you would expect to see over an old coach stop. This one either had been totally redone or was brand new. It simply said O'Meara. The letters were on the top arched over a pint of beer.

We crossed the street and went in. If it had looked drab on the outside, it was even worse inside. The floor was cement or stone. It was too dark to really tell. There were three old men seated around a wobbly table in the corner. One looked up as we came in and smiled. He hadn't a tooth in his head. Patrick apparently knew him, and waved back. All of the men were dressed in suit coats that had been bought decades ago. They didn't appear to have been to the cleaners since. One man, the furthest away, held his beer cupped in his hands. They were huge hands. His massive fingers were intertwined around the glass. Patrick could see me staring at his hands. "Those fellas are all dairy farmers, Colleen. They hand milked their cows for many years. All the older farmers in the area have hands like theirs. Actually even the younger fellas have massive hands. Farming's very hard work indeed."

There was an even older man behind the bar. He was a tiny person with no discernible expression on his face. He calmly watched us go around the end of the short bar and pass into another room. I couldn't believe my eyes. We were in a room four times the size of the bar in front. It looked like a movie set or something a designer had put together as the typical Irish bar. Three walls were lined with booths made of dark wood and leather. The far wall was a very long bar backed with an equally long mirror. It was about a third full. I felt Patrick watching me. I turned to see him smiling.

"Did I surprise you?"

"You certainly did. This is amazing, just like the bookstore in Dublin." A young woman, holding menus pressed against her bosom came up to us. "Will I find you a seat for dinner? she asked.

"Please," answered Patrick. She led the way to a booth halfway along the outside wall. We sat, and she handed each of us a menu. That done, she left. She hadn't told us her name, or asked if we would start with a drink, but she had smiled a friendly welcome. "The food is not very complicated, Colleen, but it is done very well indeed."

"Thanks Patrick." I opened my menu. The left side had fixed price dinners none more than fifteen pounds Irish. The right side was A La Carte. It looked a little more expensive than the left side. I looked down the list. There were fish entries, pork, and lamb. "Patrick, I think I'll have the roast pork with potatoes and vegetables. It comes with a desert, but I think I'll skip that. It also lists eggs mayonnaise as a starter. What's that?"

"It's just boiled eggs split and covered with mayonnaise."

"Sounds dreadful."

"It is. You know, the pork sounds good. I'll have that. I don't think I'll have a starter. Do you see anything else on the menu, Colleen?"

"No, well the...no. I'll skip the starter too. The

main course should be enough."

"It is indeed. Wasn't I here no more than a month ago, and had the pork. It was excellent then. The place is fairly new, you know. At least this part of it is. A husband and wife bought it from the old man who was behind the bar in the front. That part is the how it has been for a very long time. Back here is where the snugs were."

"Snugs, what are they?"

"Snugs are booths where the women sat. The men would drink with their cronies away from the ladies. That all started disappearing in the fifties. Anyway, the couple that bought the place were raised in Buttevant, married and moved to Dublin. They both worked in the restaurant trade, but, I think, grew tired of city life. They bought this from old Twomey out front, and agreed to keep the front bar for him. They then renovated and enlarged the snugs and installed a modern kitchen. The husband cooks, and the wife runs the restaurant. They have more business than they can handle. The food is plain, what the people around here want, but done very well, and it is good value."

I looked around the room. There was a woman directing one of the waitresses. I took her to be the owner. As I watched another girl came out of the back. She seemed to be another waitress. Maybe she was just coming on to work. It was busier now. In the little while that we had been here it had started to fill. The girl that had seated us came up to the new girl, said something and motioned in our direction. The new girl came over with as friendly a smile as the first girl's.

"Now, are you ready to order." She asked Patrick

directly. Not including me at all. I wasn't sure if I liked this much. But, I had to remember I was in a different country, and men were treated as if they were in charge, even if they weren't.

"We'll both have the pork dinner. The one from the fixed price menu please. Colleen will you have anything to drink?"

"Just water, Patrick. Thank you."

"The lady will have water, and I'll have a pint, if you please."

"Very good, sir." She then smiled at me, picked up the menus and left for the kitchen. We sat quietly. Patrick fidgeting away. He looked up at me, and then away, then back. He definitely had something to say, and didn't know how to start. I didn't help one little bit. I had a pretty good idea what was coming, and wished he would just leave it alone. Finally he stopped squirming and sat calmly. He reached over and took my hand, squeezed it, smiled at me, and released my hand. He didn't say a word, thank God. Finally our dinner came. I was glad for the distraction, but a little disappointed that his apology was not forthcoming. Maybe he wasn't going to apologize for his outburst in Dublin. Maybe I just wished he would. Well I was not to know. He seemed quite calm now.

We dug into our meals. It wasn't at all like dining at Longueville, but the food, in it's own way was every bit as good. The pork roast was very tender, browned on the outside with almost a crust. Generous portions of slices of the meat were carefully arranged along one side of a mountain of creamy mashed potatoes. The whole of that was set in a plate of natural brown pork gravy with a hint of rosemary and bay. On a side plate was a brilliant green vegetable that I had never seen before. It appeared to have been stir-fried quickly. I could see the heat waves rising off the plate. The waitress had brought a large basket of Irish Soda Bread and two tubs of butter. I felt like a farmhand eating his supper the way I roared through the meal. I had to stop and wipe my face with my napkin continuously. I was afraid that there was a river of gravy running down my face. There wasn't, but it was that kind of dinner. Patrick seemed to have taken the same approach. He was faster than I though, since he didn't have to stop to change hands as he cut his meat like I did.

Finally I finished. I repressed an urge to let out a giant belch, and sat back like a cat that has just finished off a quart of cream. I looked over at Patrick. He was watching me with a contented smile on his face. He had a milk mustache from the Guinness he had drunk. He must have guessed from my stare, so he wiped his mouth with his napkin. "Now, Colleen, would you say that was a proper meal?"

"I most certainly would. We would call that family dining in America. That was delicious and very, very filling. The vegetable they served was very good, very crisp. I haven't eaten it before. What was it?"

"Broccoli. You don't have broccoli back in the states?"

"Sure we do. That wasn't broccoli. Broccoli looks like green cauliflower. Its not leafy like this."

"I see. We have two kinds of broccoli. The one you ate here, which is really broccoli rabe, and then the kind you're used to. I think this is my favorite of the two."

"It certainly is my favorite, even though I've only had it this once. I can't stand the other stuff. Would you excuse me for a moment, Patrick? I'd like to go powder my nose."

"Of course."

When I returned Patrick had paid the bill. He was chatting with the waitress, but when he saw me he came over and we went out the side door, which led into an alley. We walked up the alley, crossed the street, and drove back to Glantane. We parked in between the two houses. Patrick said he'd pick me up in a bit, gave a cheery was as he went into Cliona's. I went into Dad's to get ready for the Hooley, not at all sure what to wear.

CHAPTER 26

Patrick hadn't really described the Hooley. I was sure it wouldn't require anything fancy, but I didn't want to look like a flash American either. Finally I put on a plain dark blue skirt, a white blouse with a high lace neck, and a red v-neck sweater. I heard a knock on the door as I pulled the sweater over my head.

"Hang on," I yelled at whoever had knocked. "Just come in I won't be a moment." I ran a brush through my hair. In the drawing room I found Patrick. He was pacing the length of the room, apparently anxious to be going. "Did I keep you Patrick?"

"Not at all. I am only nervous."

"What about?"

"I've no idea. Perhaps that my expectations for tonight won't be met? Or it could be you."

"Me? Why would I make you nervous?"

"You? Well I think, uh... no, just leave it. Probably it's no more than too much coffee today. I'll be quite all right, I'm sure."

"Let's go then I'm ready. I'll grab my coat on the way out." Patrick stepped in front of me, grabbed my coat and held it up for me to put on. As I slipped into the coat he stepped in front of me and opened the front door. "My aren't we gallant tonight." There was an edge to my voice that made my comment sound more sarcastic than I intended. In fact I was trying to be complimentary, not sarcastic. He gave me a strange look, and walked to the car. I could see the doubt in his eyes as he debated whether or not to open the car door for me. Irish hospitality ruled in the end, and he walked around the car and opened the door. "Thanks Patrick," I said, as humbly as I could manage. He seemed to cheer up at that, and sort of bounced around the car to his side.

The car zipped down the hill and turned left in the village. This was going to be new country for me, but I wouldn't see much of it at night. Patrick's rough, quick driving kept me awake until we reached the main highway. Again we turned left and headed west. There was very little other traffic on the road. Occasionally a truck would go by at a frightening rate of speed. No sooner had I started to doze off than the road would narrow, and the car would pitch from side to side. We went along this way for quite some time, me almost falling asleep, narrow road and lurching, road widening, me almost falling asleep, and so on a half a dozen times. Finally at what seemed to be a low spot in the hedge we turned right. We proceeded up a very narrow lane that I could never have spotted, even in full daylight. Eventually we came to a village, and turned left just before entering the village. The road climbed a bit and then where it turned left we turned right up a small track that was lined with cars. Men with lanterns were spaced along the track. They directed us to a spot in a field where cars were being parked.

It was hard to see much. The night was dark. There were no streetlights only the lanterns and the lights of parking cars that were quickly switched off. Back along the track I could see a very small two-story house where everyone seemed to be going. Patrick pulled the car beside another, and we got out. We joined the other people trekking through the field towards the lit house in the distance. If we could have viewed this scene it probably would have looked like a Turner painting, not a particular one, but the light must have been something like his "London Fire," or was it "London Bridge." I couldn't remember. We continued our moth like approach until we could hear the music from inside.

"This will be a fierce night, altogether." Patrick had turned towards me as he made this proclamation. The enthusiasm in his face, and in his voice was infectious. I gave his arm a squeeze and smiled at him. He squeezed back and we went into the tiny house. We found ourselves in an entry not much bigger than us. Ahead was a narrow stair going up. A room was to the right, which was filled with women carting trays of drink in and out. To our left was another door, a very narrow door, with a great deal of noise coming from the other side. Patrick carefully opened the door and we went in. The room was packed. It was filled with the most varied collection of people I had ever seen. Priests, farmers, business people, Nuns, old people, kids, and every age between, all in a room no bigger than 15 feet a side.

Right in front of us two young men were seated on a bench. They were miming some kind of sewing and singing as they sewed. Quite a few people were watching them, but there were many knots of people discussing whatever with each other. I couldn't quite understand what the two men were singing while they sowed. So I asked Patrick. "They're singing in Irish, Colleen. It is an "amhrán sothair," a work song."

As I watched I could see that whatever they were saying was matched with very intricate movements. It fascinated me. The movements, coupled with the singing in Irish, were very hypnotic. I didn't notice that a very large man had turned from the crowd of people watching the performance and come over to my side. Patrick startled me with his introduction. "Colleen, I would like you to meet Padraig O' hIceadha, he is the host of these wonderful gatherings." A very large, tall man stood at my side. He took my hand with both of his and smiled a welcome. "You are very welcome. I hope you find something to interest you tonight." I didn't know which was more impressive, the size of his hard hands or the warmth of his smile. "Perhaps, later tonight, you can tell us all, why you came to Ireland, or perhaps you have a poem you'd like to recite."

"Padraig," chimed in Patrick, "Colleen's Father was murdered at Dromineen last week." I could see the embarrassment creep onto his face. The smile crumbled, and he squeezed my hand a little harder. "I am so sorry for your troubles miss. I can be quite insensitive. Please forgive me. Will I fetch you a punch?" Without waiting for a reply he went over to one of the ladies handing out small glasses of drink. He took one glass, which disappeared into his fist and returned. "Now, by way of amends," Padraig said as he handed me the small glass. He excused himself and turned to another group of people. Patrick was watching me closely with the start of a smile playing on his mouth. I was trying to figure out what was amusing him so much when I took a slug of the punch. As soon as the liquid hit my throat I knew the source of Patrick's smile. I started to choke, but quickly recovered. It was sweet, lemony whiskey. This wasn't punch it was a hot toddy.

"Sorry, Colleen. I couldn't resist."

"That's a fine way to treat a guest." I wasn't angry. I would have most likely done the same. What a surprise. The drink actually tasted good. While Patrick was smirking, I continued looking around the room. In an alcove in the far corner were three middle-aged men sitting on a couch. They looked pretty much straight ahead with little expression on their face. "Patrick who are those men over there. The ones on the couch." Patrick turned to where I was looking. "What's wrong. They don't seem to be quite right. All of them are kind of staring off into space?" Patrick chuckled. "They're totally pissed. These fellows are all bachelors that live for these hooleys. They know all of the old songs and will sing many of them tonight. It is a sight worth seein. Maybe I should have said a sound worth hearing? Colleen would you mind if I left you on your own for a bit? I see the lady I came to see over with Father O'Rian."

"Go right ahead, Patrick. I'll just watch all the activity." Patrick walked over to a little old lady who was talking to a priest. The working song had finished, and an accordion started up behind me. Padraig was gently herding people away from the center of the room. Soon four couples came to the center of the room and began to square dance, sort of, except there wasn't a caller. Everyone was watching the spirited dance, well, almost everyone. I could see Patrick deep in conversation with the lady he had come to see. The rest of us were engrossed in the music and the couples dancing.

I was disappointed when the dancing stopped. But no sooner was it done than one of the men sitting on the couch stood up and began singing in the clearest tenor I have ever heard. I couldn't make out the words very well, but his voice was sweet and pure. It made the hair on my neck stand on end. "The boys of Barr na Sriada, I think it's called," said a voice behind me. I turned to see a tall gaunt man with a fixed smile on his face. "Please allow me to introduce myself," he said. "I am the Reverend Samuels. I was most distressed to learn of your father's death, my condolences."

"Thank you Reverend," I responded. I couldn't make out his accent. He really didn't sound Irish, at least not like anyone I'd heard yet. "It's very kind of you. My name is Colleen O'Donovan," I said as I stuck out my hand to be shaken. He stared at my hand, not quite sure what to do. Eventually he took the tips of my fingers in his hand, and smiled a thin smile as he wiggled my fingers. "Come let's sit over there', he suggested. We walked over to two chairs that had just been vacated by the musicians. "Now, how do you like our little show?

"I think it's marvelous. There are so many talented people."

"Talented? Well I suppose in there own little way they are talented. I do wish they wouldn't use so much Irish. I find it indecipherable. Enough of that, though. How are you faring?"

"I think I'm doing fine, all things being considered. The Murphys have been very kind. In fact everyone has been very kind, almost everyone. Cliona and Patrick took me to Dublin, which helped a lot. It was a very interesting trip."

"I am particularly fond of Dublin. I would like very much to live there myself, but duty keeps me in Mallow. What did you find that made Dublin so interesting?

"I was in the most marvelous bookstore in the world. Room after room of books, with a marvelous cafe in the center. Maybe the most amazing thing about the bookstore was the fact that it looked like nothing from the outside. We stayed in what I think was a remodeled stable in the South of Dublin that was very attractive. Everything was enjoyable about the trip, well almost everything. If it hadn't of been for the Superintendent the whole trip would have been fabulous."

"The Superintendent, miss? You don't mean our own Superintendent Mundell, do you?"

"Yes I do. What a very strange man to follow me all the way to Dublin, for God knows what purpose. He suspects me of the Donal Kelly murder, I'm afraid."

"He can't possibly. That makes no sense whatsoever."

"I agree, but I can't think of any other reason why he would follow me to Dublin. And then when he sees me to simply turn and walk away. It really doesn't make any sense. Although Patrick had a theory that he himself is the murderer"

"Strange, yes very strange indeed. Leaving that for the moment how is your stay here? Have you done anything interesting?

"No not really. Mostly I've just hung around Cliona and Patrick waiting for something to happen about Dad's murder. I just... you know I did find something out of the ordinary, or so Patrick thinks. When Patrick and I were down at Dromineen castle I found the entrance to an underground tunnel. Maybe that's what it was anyway. Patrick thought it might have something to do with the battle of Knocknanuss. What's wrong Reverend? You look very strange?"

"Nothing, Colleen, nothing at all. Just allow me to regain my composure. There! I'm quite all right I can assure you. It's just that I had a fright when you told me about the tunnel. You see... Oh dear this is very distressing indeed. I'm afraid that perhaps Patrick may be correct about the Inspector."

"Correct? You mean he may have killed my Father?"

"I'm afraid so. I told the inspector about the tunnel not too long ago, and I told him that it was possibly connected with the battle of Knocknanuss."

"But how does that connect him with the murder? I don't see what that has to do with Dad."

"I also told your Father."

Oh! But why would he care?"

"Well it was all connected with bagpipes and the battle of Knocknanuss. Probably your Father was investigating the tunnel when the Superintendent came upon him. There must be something in that tunnel that implicates the Superintendent. He probably hasn't had a chance to retrieve it. I think we should go right now and find out what it is before it is too late."

"Right now?"

"Yes just wait while I tell Patrick where we've gone."

I sat thinking about what he had said. If Dad had gone to the cave to research the paper he was working on, and had discovered or actually interrupted the Superintendent doing something there, the Superintendent could have killed him to keep him quiet. Dad wouldn't have expected any trouble and had probably been caught unawares. I looked over to see the Reverend leaning over Patrick. Patrick was saying something to him, but I couldn't hear. The Reverend stood up and came back over to where I was sitting. Patrick had turned back to the lady he was talking to.

"Are you ready Colleen? I explained to Patrick. He seemed to think it was a good idea if we left immediately. He said he would follow as soon as he finished talking to Mrs. Hickey."

"I'm ready, lets go." As we were leaving Liam came in the front door. "Hi Liam. I didn't expect to see you tonight."

"Hello Colleen. Are you coming back? Vicar, good evening"

"Mr.Lenihan, good night."

"I'm not sure how long we'll be gone Liam. Patrick's over there. He can explain we're in a bit of a hurry." The Vicar rushed me out the door, leaving Liam with a puzzled expression on his face.

CHAPTER 27

Molly how are you keeping?"

"I've no complaints that great beauty wouldn't cure. And how's your care?"

"Mother is doing well. She is timeless, I think. Each day a new adventure. I cannot keep up, I know. I have been looking forward to this evening for weeks Molly. I've fairly well exhausted the libraries. They all say about the same thing. Although, when I was in Dublin I may have found something interesting"

"Dublin, Libraries! Patrick you should have come to me. Between Seorse, Con, and meself there is ten times the knowledge of that battle than is in all the libraries of the world. Did you know that Seorse passed on, poor divil. And there were questions."

"Oh no Molly. I hadn't heard. There was little about Duhallow that he didn't know. What do you mean by circumstances? Was he murdered?"

"No, not at all. I've said more than enough as it is. Father Bowler has seen to it that he is to get a proper Christian Burial. Now! We've written out the history of the battle as it's been passed down in our family. I have a copy for you. Padraig wanted a copy for <u>Seanchas Duhallow</u> so I gave it to him and he made a few copies on one of those machines. Will I give you one?"

"Oh yes, thank you. I very much want to read this. Could you tell some of it, the main points as it were."

"I can, of course. I'll start with.... Hello Vicar."

"Hello Molly. Patrick I think I might be able to help Colleen with her Father's murder. We are just going to the place she found the other night. She asked if you would join us when you are through here."

"I will of course Vicar. I'll follow as soon as Molly and I are finished."

"Very well, we'll not wait."

"Sorry Molly, could you start again?"

I can, but you watch yourself with the Vicar."

"With the Vicar? Why"

"Just you listen to my story. I'll be quick. I think you should go to the young lady quickly. In fact I'll only tell you the part that you haven't found in the history books. Well, it seems that three days before the battle the O'Reillys attacked Rinnucini's baggage train and stole all the funds that were to be used to feed the Confederacy soldiers. We went into battle without having eaten for three days. We fought valiantly and almost carried the day, but in the late afternoon our energy waned, and in the end we lost to Inchquin. Now, according to my family's memory of the event, Allisdare McDonnell was captured and led away his hands bound to his reins. We also, well my cousin's family also, think that Taafe was not at the battle at all, but sat drinking tea at Assolas house. You won't find that in the history books."

"Where was I? Oh yes, they led McDonnell off with Lord Inchquin's retinue. As they came to a stream

McDonnell's horse bent down to drink from the stream. As the horse bent over it pulled McDonnell over exposing his back through a break in his armor. One of the sycophants that followed the English around ran his sword into McDonnell back killing him. Now, this is the most interesting part. Yes the most interesting indeed." Molly leaned over very close and put her finger alongside her nose. "That man's name was Samuels. The Vicar is his direct descendent. Now the place that you two discovered, is it the cave below Dromineen where McDonnell is buried?"

"I think it is Molly. Why do you ask?"

"The Samuels have been stealing from their church for centuries. They hide their booty under the castle. Now, I told all of this to the young ladies father. He was asking about the use of bagpipes at the battle for something he was writing. I know little of such things, but thought this story would be interesting. I think he must have discovered the cave, and the Vicar found out and committed murder. Your young lady is in trouble I think. She could end up the same as her Da, and you as well if you're not careful."

"I'm astounded Molly. Why haven't you told anyone before this?"

"Didn't I try to see the Superintendent many times? He hadn't any use for me at all. You'd best be off now."

"Yes I'd better. I'll grab Liam and have him follow me there. Thank you Molly?"

"Not at all." But be off quickly. There's murder in the air I fear.

CHAPTER 28

We were traveling at a good rate of speed. In fact, we were flying. The Vicar seemed intent on getting to Dromineen as quickly as possible. His slightly unctuous manner had disappeared, and he was totally taciturn. I couldn't get a word out of him. If I hadn't traveled this road many times with Patrick driving like a bat out of hell, I might have been concerned. The Vicar was not a great driver, but he wasn't going as fast as Patrick had gone. So I settled back quite content to leave the driving to him, or at least to his agent. The car teetered back and forth as we thundered down the road, the car lights bouncing madly along the hedgerows. Finally we came careening to a stop at the gate across the entrance to Donal's property.

The Vicar silently left the car, hurried around to my side and opened the door. As I started to get out of the car he grabbed my hand and almost pulled me over in his haste to get going. "Vicar! You needn't pull me all the way there. I'm quite capable of self propulsion." My ascerbic wit never ceased to astonish me.

We climbed the fence and half ran down the field to the castle. Only when we passed the castle and started down the hill to the water did the Vicar slow down. He went directly to where the grate that I had found was located. He moved the bushes quickly and opened the grate. I couldn't see where the gate was until he had it opened. Even though I had just been there. Very roughly he pulled me inside. Not a word had passed his lips. It was very strange. Once inside the opening we appeared to be inside a natural limestone cavern that was about five feet high. Both of us were bent over when all of a sudden we were in a vaulted chamber. The roof was at least ten feet in height. Three of the walls had many niches cut into them. The fourth wall had a stout wooden door right in the center. "Behold the burial chamber of the Kings of the O'Callaghans." I started at the voice of the Vicar. He was confident now, in charge. He had a look of contempt on his face as he turned pointing his flashlight at each of the walls.

"Come my dear, and I will show you the rarest of sights." With this he turned and walked to the heavy wooden door. He drew a large key from his coat, inserted it into the keyhole in the door, turned the key, silently, and opened the door. The Vicar went in. He turned halfway through the door, and gestured to me to follow. I was fascinated. I didn't see how any of this had anything to do with Dad's murder, but I couldn't wait to see what he had in that room. Well I should have waited. I should have waited forever.

As soon as I got into the room he lit a torch that was mounted in a sconce in the wall. I couldn't believe my eyes. The room was full of treasure. There were paintings stacked against one wall. The center of the room was filled with chests. There were bureaus with god knows what, in them. I heard the Vicar snicker behind me. I turned to see him shutting the door. This was getting even stranger. "What is all this Vicar? And what does it have to do with Dad? I thought you said there might be some clues about his murder."

"Indeed I did state that. Did I not? I was, I think, less than honest with you. This room is not, after all, a clue in your father's murder, but the reason for his death. Now, if you will please sit quietly on that chest we will wait for Patrick to arrive."

"What do you mean this room is the reason for Dad's dying. And why do you think that Patrick is coming?"

"All in good time, all in good time. Now sit!" There was such menace in his voice that I quickly sat as he had instructed. While we waited the Vicar walked along the length of the room. He would caress each of the objects that he passed lovingly. His face had a composed beatific look about it. This room held great meaning for him. I thought I could hear very soft whistling. His lips were slightly pursed, but I couldn't be sure. I wasn't frightened, not yet, anyway, but I also was not feeling too good about all of this. I just realized that there was no sign of the Superintendent. It was beginning to dawn on me that I had been brought here for reasons other than those stated. I hadn't yet figured it out, but I would soon, very soon.

Before long I heard Patrick in the room outside. "Colleen, Vicar! Are you in here? The Vicar quickly moved to the door and called Patrick into the room. He looked at me questioningly. "What's happening?" he asked. As he had come into the room the Vicar had quietly moved behind Patrick and was now standing in the doorway. "What is happening Patrick is that I now have you two bothersome people where you will create no more problems for me."

"Problems for you," we spoke in unison. "What do you mean Vicar?" asked Patrick. "This room is what I mean Patrick. This is where my family has stored what we have stolen from the Church for many centuries. Each of these items is owed to my ancestors by the Church for our sacrifices we have made in the name of the Church of Ireland these many centuries. Your discovering this room is as dangerous to me as was the young lady's father's discovery of this room."

"My father discovered this room? Is that what you meant when you said the police might have some clues they were hiding here?"

"No, not at all. I said that simply to get you to accompany me here. I seriously doubt that the police have any idea that this place exists." No your father actually discovered this room. I don't know how he found it. We have kept the entrance well hidden. Judging from his notes his research led him here. I talked to him about it once, but he feigned ignorance. When I came here one evening to, as it were, make a withdrawal, I saw your father leaving the opening. He was backing out and didn't see me approach. I didn't know what else to do you see. I had to protect the family. I picked up a large stone and hit him on the side of the head. He fell over backward down to where they found him. I climbed down and had to finish him with a couple more blows."

"You killed her father? Patrick yelled at the Vicar as he started forward. The Vicar had drawn a revolver that we hadn't noticed. He waved it at Patrick.

"I think you had better stop where you are if you care for this lady at all." Patrick froze. The Vicar had a triumphant grin on his face, as he announced, "Isn't it a saying in America, like father like son? Well I am most sorry, but I am afraid it will have to be like father like daughter, now both of you turn around."

As he said that I saw a blur of motion behind the Vicar. A shape was formed in the doorway and I heard a thud. All of a sudden I saw Liam standing over the collapsed form of the Vicar. He had a club in his hand. Both he and Patrick rushed me out of the room and out into the night air. As we came out many uniformed Garda rushed into the cavern. They rushed me off into the night.

CHAPTER 29

We were gathered in Cliona's drawing room. Cliona and I sat on the couch facing the fireplace listening to Liam and Patrick regale us with the evening's events. I was still in shock. Unsure whether I was sad for being reminded of Dad's death, afraid of almost being killed myself, or glad at finally capturing Dad's murderer. I suppose I was all three.

The Vicar, of all people. And simply because of Dad's research into the battle of Knocknanuss and what Molly had told him. "Colleen are you all right?" Cliona was very comforting. She had quickly taken me into her home and restored me with tea. We had driven back quickly, Patrick and I. Soon after Liam appeared with his notebook to ask us what had happened that night. Patrick had explained as best he could, after I had told Liam about the Vicar's approach to me at the Hooley. Cliona had told Liam to leave it until the next day, which he did after we both gave him a brief description of the evening's events. Now Patrick and Liam were explaining something about the Superintendent.

"You mean he wasn't following Colleen at all in Dublin."

"No Patrick. He is quite smitten with your mother, and apparently hoped for a chance meeting in Dublin."

"My mother, Liam?"

"Yes Patrick your mother. It would seem that he was quite taken with her when he first arrived in Mallow, but was reluctant to press his suit when he learned of her admiration for Donal Kelly, from Donal himself of course."

"But Liam why would he be interested in my... oh sorry mother. I ... oh dear my foot's in it again. All my theories about his part in the murder of Colleen's father, they are very embarrassing now. Except I don't feel very embarrassed.

"You shouldn't feel embarrassed Patrick. There was some reason to feel that he could have been the killer. By the way Novak called back. It seems that Dad had asked him to see if the Irish Superintendent they had met some years ago at a conference, was Mundell. It seemed possible at the time you explained your theory. I don't think you should feel bad about it.

"Why was the Vicar so upset by the discovery of his private cave anyway? He never explained why he thought it so dangerous, dangerous enough to kill.

"We really haven't been able to question him thoroughly yet, but I think I can describe it fairly well with what I know now. First off, his family, or rather his ancestor who murdered Alisder McDonnell was given the lands the family still holds. In addition the man was made Vicar of the Parish that our man is in charge of. It would appear that it wasn't enough. Right from the start the family started stealing. Mostly from the Church, but if other opportunities arose they took advantage. After the O'Callaghans removed the body of McDonnell from wherever Lord Inchquin had buried him they brought him to burial site of their Kings. It was close to the last act of Donough O'Callaghan, their Chief at that time, since he was transplanted to Clare by Ireton who then stole their lands. Only one of the O'Callaghan Chieftains ever came back to this area and he was killed for his trouble."

"Now this is speculation of course, but I think that the Samuels found out about the cave from one of Ireton's men. After a number of years, seeing that no O'Callaghan with any knowledge of the place had come back, they felt secure in using the cave for hiding their loot. So they began storing their booty there. As the years passed, I imagine that they felt they had to secure their collection, and built the room where the Vicar took you."

"Liam, I see that the Vicar would prefer that no one would know about the treasure, but it certainly wasn't important enough to kill for."

"Ah Patrick, in that you are wrong. It seems that the good Vicar was under suspicion by his Bishop for having pilched some of the Church funds. In fact as far as I can tell, the Bishop and he had words on the matter this very week. And, not only did they have words, but the Vicar promised that he would set everything right."

"Liam, Patrick, excuse me, but do you think I set him off?"

"What do you mean Colleen?"

"When you went off to talk to that woman at the party the Vicar joined me. I told him about the cave that I had found. He acted strangely."

"That's it, that's it indeed Colleen. You did set

him off. He must have panicked thinking that he now had another person to deal with, and very little time before it all came out. Don't you agree Liam."

"Very likely Patrick."

"Not only did I tell him that I had found it, but I told him you had too."

"So that's why he came over to me, to make sure that I followed, since he had to deal with the both of us. Well it is a good thing Molly had just told me about the cave and your Dad. I probably wouldn't have brought Liam with me if she hadn't"

"You brought Liam based on Molly's story? That seems a little far fetched."

"I suppose it was Colleen, but I have never trusted that man, not at all."

"This is all very interesting, the lot of you, but don't you think we should all get some sleep before we drop?" Cliona had, as usual, hit the nail on the head.

"Shouldn't we first find out what Colleen's plans are, mother? I am sure we all would like you to see a better side of Ireland than you have. Colleen, are you staying with us for a while?"

"Patrick I really don't know. I need to recover from the last week. I suppose I'll stay at least until all the legalities over Dad's house are settled. That should take a while I imagine. Now if you will excuse me I'm going home to get some sleep.